GREEK'S HAND IN VENGEANCE

LORRAINE HALL

PRESENTS

If you purchased this book without a cover you should be aware that this book is stolen property. It was reported as "unsold and destroyed" to the publisher, and neither the author nor the publisher has received any payment for this "stripped book."

Recycling programs for this product may not exist in your area.

ISBN-13: 978-1-335-21384-6

Greek's Hand in Vengeance

For questions and comments about the quality of this book, please contact us at CustomerService@Harlequin.com.

Harlequin Enterprises ULC
22 Adelaide St. West, 41st Floor
Toronto, Ontario M5H 4E3, Canada
www.Harlequin.com

HarperCollins Publishers
Macken House, 39/40 Mayor Street Upper,
Dublin 1, D01 C9W8, Ireland
www.HarperCollins.com

Printed in Lithuania

“Then what does it involve?”

He had considered this part carefully. For a while, he’d even planned to romance her. Convince her it was all real.

But that had felt a bit too much like leaving a victim in his wake.

Zervou believed in revenge and retribution, but he did not believe in collateral damage. Not when he had been such.

So, he went with the truth. It was its own kind of blow. Would Ari dodge it? Return her own? He couldn’t wait to find out.

“Your father.”

He watched as her entire body stilled with tension. She tried to remain relaxed on the outside, but something about the word *father* certainly surprised her. If they were boxing, he’d have landed a blow.

So he added the rest, a one-two punch, so to speak. “And revenge.”

Her chin came up. Her eyes flashing. Ready to deliver the return blow. He found himself smiling.

“I do not have a father,” she said flatly.

He did love a spar. “Then I suppose the name Erjon Hyseni means nothing to you.”

He could see it flash in her eyes. She knew. Which made his plan that much easier to implement.

Lorraine Hall is a part-time hermit and full-time writer. She was born with an old soul and her head in the clouds, which, it turns out, is the perfect combination to spend her days creating thunderous alpha heroes and the fierce, determined heroines who win their hearts. She lives in a potentially haunted house with her soulmate and rambunctious band of hermits-in-training. When she's not writing romance, she's reading it.

Books by Lorraine Hall

Harlequin Presents

A Wedding Between Enemies
Pregnant, Stolen, Wed
Unwrapping His Forbidden Assistant

The Diamond Club

Italian's Stolen Wife

Rebel Princesses

His Hidden Royal Heirs
Princess Bride Swap

Work Wives to Billionaires' Wives

The Bride Wore Revenge

Babies for Royal Brides

Secretly Pregnant Princess
King's Heir Ultimatum

Visit the Author Profile page at Harlequin.com.

GREEK'S HAND IN VENGEANCE

For the fighters

CHAPTER ONE

ZERVOU KRITIKOS MOVED THROUGH the dim, grimy boxing gym with a singular focus that had led him to where he was in life: From the boy who'd lost his comfortable childhood at the age of ten, struggled to save his mother after his father was murdered in front of them, into an adolescent and then a man who had worked toward success every second of every day since.

He *was* successful now, rich beyond even his wildest dreams, and no doors were shut to him anymore. Ever. He had everything he could possibly want.

Except the destruction of one final enemy.

But this was the year he would finally ferret Erjon Hyseni out of his hiding and destroy the man who'd killed his father.

Some called it hearsay that Erjon was the hitman who'd sought revenge on the Kritikos family for not caving to the thugs and mobsters that infiltrated their tiny Greek village all those years ago. Zervou knew it for what it was: the simple truth. Regardless of the details, Erjon had killed his father and that had sentenced his mother to a life of pain. So, no, details did not matter.

Simple truths required retribution.

Zervou had gone on to save his village from the criminals who had once run it, never quite managing to get his hands on the slippery Erjon. Still, Anovol was now a small, thriving community with an almost miniscule crime rate. That success had brought him solace for a while, but Erjon remained out of his reach, gallivanting around Europe as a member of the Petrov crime family.

It had taken some years, and accumulating some wealth, for Zervou to begin to close in on Erjon and enact his revenge. He had managed to stop most of the Petrov family, but Erjon had managed to escape—going into hiding almost a decade ago. A hiding even Zervou had not been able to find.

So Zervou had spent these years mining the depths of Erjon's past. And in this he had finally found the one secret he felt he could use against Erjon, the one secret that would pull this weasel out of his hiding place and put him into jail. Forever.

The existence of a daughter.

A daughter Zervou was quite certain no one besides Erjon and the mother knew about. Except now *him*.

He approached the man behind the counter. The gym was dimly lit, smelled exactly like what it was and was not the kind of place Zervou lingered these days. In any other circumstance, he would have sent one of his men to bring the woman to him. He lived far above anything that might remind him of the scrabbling teenage existence he'd left behind.

But he had to be sure this would work, so he came himself, with his men flanking him, so that no one might mistake him for *belonging* here in this poor area of Corfu.

He gestured for one of his men to address the desk attendant now. Zervou might need to see this woman for himself, but that did not mean he would be doing the dirty work. He kept his hands clean these days.

"We are looking for Ariadne Malis," Bacchus—one of Zervou's most trusted assistants—informed the man who wore a T-shirt advertising the boxing gym's name. He did not look like much of a boxer, and his expression was one of pure boredom.

The attendant looked them up and down. Then shrugged. "Ari's in the ring," he told them, pointing deeper into the gym where muffled sounds of thuds and grunts were coming from.

Zervou gave him a magnanimous nod before moving with his men beyond the front desk into the bowels of the gym.

Punching bags of all kinds hung in different areas, and mats littered the ground. A handful of men were at all the different stations, but at the center of it all was a decently constructed ring, and two people fighting in it.

It was easy enough to pick out his target. One of the boxers was a man. The other the woman he was looking for.

Pleased with the timing of getting to see her at work, Zervou crossed his arms over his chest and watched.

She wore headgear that hid most of her face, but her body was bared in brief shorts and sports bra. Muscles rippled with every move—a dodge, a punch, a bounce—sweat made her olive skin glisten under the ugly fluorescent light.

Fascinating. She moved not just as an athlete. She was an artist. A dancer. Powerful with it, but it was not *all* power. There was a grace and canniness behind every move. She dodged two quick punches, one just barely missing her chin, then delivered a blow right to the man's stomach.

He stumbled back, then held up a hand. It must have been some kind of surrender, because when they came together at the center of the mat again, they shook hands before retreating to their corners.

Ariadne lowered herself onto a stool, unwrapped her hands, then took off the soft helmet she'd been wearing. Underneath the helmet, her dark hair was pinned in tight plaits against her scalp. She was breathing heavily and clearly taking a few moments to gather herself despite what had to have been some kind of practice victory.

Though she did not look at him, there was no doubt her dark eyes took in the trio of men in suits watching her. But he liked that she did not rush to greet them and find out who they were or what they were here for.

She would do this on her own time.

"She is perfect," Zervou said to both men. "I will be at the car. Bring her to me when she is ready." Then, without another look back, Zervou left the gym.

Certain this was the beginning of everything he'd been waiting for.

Ari focused on the routine she used after every practice bout: rehash with her sparring partner and their coach, stretch, shower and change into her street clothes. She did not rush through it, even knowing those men were waiting for her.

She had learned early and well that if she let men set the pace of her life, she would end up at the bottom of their shoe. She would be scraped off no one's boot in this lifetime. Never again.

At first when the three men had arrived, she'd wondered if her father's threats had finally come to call. She'd nearly taken a jab to the chin for the distraction. She'd quickly dismissed it, getting back into her fight. She might have *hoped* it was her father's henchmen, but the tallest man was too recognizable.

Zervou Kritikos was well-known in Corfu these days—probably well-known across Europe, though Ari's life was small and existed in the city limits of her hometown. Her entire life was this boxing gym, the modest apartment she shared with her mother and not much else.

Kritikos's company was some kind of stadium business. Ari had never paid much mind to what exactly they did. She just knew that what had begun with building music venues had recently expanded into sport. Something she knew the owner of the boxing gym hoped would include hosting boxing matches once it was completed.

Ari had not come to boxing for money or fame. She had come to save herself. And fallen in love with a brutal sport that would eventually be too brutal to continue. There was something about the ephemeral nature of it all—a young person's game that you either gave up or it ate you up—that appealed to Ari's fatalistic view of life.

Because her life was a series of hourglasses slowly running out. Her father would not be in hiding forever.

Some day, I will return. And everything you are will be owned by me.

She had not responded to her father's threat at the time—she'd still had hope that her obedience might save her mother back then. But inwardly she had promised herself one thing.

Never.

But whoever these men today were, it was not Erjon come to collect. So, she supposed she needed to face it head-on.

Now dressed, she hefted her duffel on her shoulder and was unsurprised to find two large men in clearly expensive suits and dark glasses waiting for her right outside the locker room door.

One was concealing a gun. The other was not. Ari always made sure to clock a man's weapons against her.

She looked up at the men blocking her way. Not with belligerence. Belligerence often spoke of weakness, and Ari was confident in her own strength. She knew her place in the world. So she looked at these men with boredom. "Is there a reason you two are standing in my way like hulking statues?" she asked pleasantly enough.

The two men exchanged glances. "You will come with us."

"And why would I do that?"

"I am sure you saw who watched your fight."

"Many people like to watch me fight." She flashed them a grin. "I'm quite exciting."

Neither of them betrayed so much as a flicker of annoyance.

"Mr. Kritikos has a business proposition to present you, if you will come with us."

Ari considered being difficult. She enjoyed being difficult when the moment called for it. She could pretend she didn't know who Mr. Kritikos was. Pretend she wasn't interested.

But a woman in her position couldn't always afford to pretend. Knowing that Mr. Kritikos was expanding into sport meant this was likely about boxing, which meant she would listen to his *business proposition*. Didn't mean she had to take it. She made a gesture toward the front of the gym. "After you, gentlemen."

That almost got the flicker of a frown out of the taller one. She'd consider that a success.

They led her out of the gym and into a sparkling, sunny afternoon. The briny air was much warmer than when she'd walked in to train before the sun had come up.

The two suited men had to be sweltering, but they led her to where Zervou Kritikos stood next to a shiny car she was no doubt meant to be impressed by. But Ari knew nothing about cars or whatever designer labels he was likely wearing.

She knew about boxing and survival.

And men. Though she mostly boxed other women in actual bouts, often her training partners were men. She spent an unreasonable amount of time in male-dominated spaces, even if there were other female boxers about.

Still, Zervou Kritikos standing here on the grimy street in front of a boxing gym seemed all wrong. He was…like a myth, this titan of industry with more money than her entire ancestral line had probably ever seen put together. He seemed like someone who would turn to dust just by walking down a street in an area such as this. People spit on the streets here, stumbled drunk down alleys, committed unspeakable crimes.

People did not drive fancy cars or wear clothes that probably cost more than she'd made in her entire life. People did not stand with such innate confidence that this show of wealth and power would not be challenged. Everyone in this neighborhood was a fighter, whether they boxed or not.

She supposed he looked like he *could* fight. Even the elegant lines of his suit could not hide the broad shoulders, the powerful stature meant to intimidate. His dark eyes were astute and assessing, with a sharp, aristocratic nose and lips arranged into some kind of knowing but vaguely amused curve.

He was outrageously handsome. She had no doubt he graced tabloids and magazine covers and had a whole slew of people aflutter over all that rich-guy appeal.

Ari knew better than to find herself aflutter over a man, wealthy or otherwise, no matter how good he looked. But there he stood, and no matter how confident she was in her ability to handle men, something about the mythical nature of his visage had her considering if she knew how to handle *that*.

"Ariadne Malis," he greeted in a voice low and powerful. "You are quite the boxer."

She said nothing to this statement. It was true. So she felt it required no response.

"I would like to extend an invitation for you to dine with me this evening."

So predictable. No matter how he looked, he was still a man. *Business propositions* never really meant honest business, did they?

Ari had to force herself not to roll her eyes. She kept her smile bland. He was likely the kind of man who never heard the word *no*. "And I would like to pass."

His lips curved, not into anything as bland as a smile. No, Ari did not have the words for this man's innate power and appeal and the way he knew how to arrange his features in just the right way to have her heart fluttering unsteadily in her chest.

When her heart *never* fluttered.

"You have no curiosity about why I would extend such an invitation?"

She looked him up and down, made sure her own features were arranged to look disappointed—though she could hardly be. "None."

He made a considering sound, and that dark, intense gaze of his held her pinned to a spot as powerfully as any grapple hold.

She had been ogled in many a different way—out of interest, a need to prove power or might, just straight-up desire for violence. But whatever *this* was, she didn't recognize it.

She scowled against that feeling. The softening of something inside her, a rearranging of her walls and the strong protections that kept them intact.

This man was dangerous, and yet it was not a danger she had any experience fighting. It was an off-putting experience. She didn't want to like it, but… Well, she was intrigued.

"I assure you, Ms. Malis, this meeting will be very worth your while."

Worth your while was hard to ignore, especially coming from a man who clearly had worth to spare. Nevertheless, she should say no and walk away. There were some lines she wouldn't cross, even for survival.

Still, she said nothing and stayed put.

"I will send a car. Here or your home. Take your pick.

All you have to do is dine with me, listen to my proposition, then give me an answer."

"And if my answer is no, you'll take it? Because you do not strike me as a man who takes no for an answer."

His eyes gleamed with satisfaction. "An excellent judge of character, Ms. Malis. But for you? Should you really reject my proposal?" He shrugged, clearly not considering it a possibility. "I'll take no for an answer. After a fashion."

After a fashion. She narrowly resisted rolling her eyes again. She also didn't say the words she needed to. Because instead of *no*, she said, "I can't imagine I have anything suitable in my wardrobe to dine with you, Mr. Kritikos."

"No need to concern yourself with wardrobe or anything else. How about this? I'll pay you for the meeting. Consider it a…listening fee." He named a sum, not outrageous, but certainly hard to refuse if all she had to do was have dinner with the man.

She had been scrabbling to keep a roof over her and her mother's head for too long to fall for something too good to be true, but it also made it hard to outright refuse the possibility for *something.* This man was richer than God, so certainly there was a possibility here.

But…wasn't she smarter than this?

"Surely you're not afraid," Zervou said with some censure in his tone. "I saw you fight in there. You should fear nothing."

"A smart woman knows there is always something to fear. Especially from charming men in expensive suits." And because she was good at sizing up an opponent, she knew the suit could not hide just how sleek and strong he was under the expensive garment. She could take him—she had the training to take down bigger and stronger opponents—but that didn't mean it'd be an easy task or one she wanted to test, particularly considering his hulking bodyguards.

Men like him didn't fight fair.

"Ah, so you think I am charming." He straightened the lapels of his suit jacket. "And stylish."

It should not have been amusing, this arrogance, but it turned out that, with a man who embodied such rugged good looks along with wealth and power, it was hard not to be a little amused.

And charmed.

"Very well," he said on a sigh, as if he was giving into some demand she'd made when she'd said nothing. "Here is the address—travel by your own means." He held out a card. "No need to worry about your wardrobe. It will be a private affair. Arm yourself however you wish."

He did not make a move to hand her the card. He simply held it out. Like holding a treat to a dog and waiting for it to approach.

She should be offended. She should turn and walk away. She should do a lot of things.

But the amount of money he'd mentioned kept playing in her head. Taking the card didn't mean she had to go. It just gave her some time to consider what kind of risks she was willing to take. Risks were part of life. Part of survival, that was for certain. Taking the card was no risk.

Chin up, shoulders relaxed, she stepped forward and plucked the card out of his fingers, making certain to avoid even the brush of fingertips. "I'll think about it," she said, and began to walk away from the trio of men.

Down the street, toward her apartment building just around the corner.

Mr. Kritikos offered no parting shot, no farewell.

But she could feel his eyes follow her the entire walk down the street.

CHAPTER TWO

CORFU GLITTERED LIKE a jewel down the glowing coast as Zervou waited for his dinner companion. The air was salty and sweet, everything around him quiet. It was a relaxing counterpoint to his usual type of estate.

He had bought this one with the sole excuse to woo Ariadne into his plan, but perhaps he would keep it even after. Most of the properties he owned he had chosen for their proximity to a bustling, exciting nightlife. Zervou liked to keep himself busy.

Perhaps age was creeping upon him as everyone had always warned if he was suddenly interested in *peace* for the first time.

But there would be no peace until the germ of Erjon Hyseni was rotting in a jail cell for the rest of his days.

Zervou had a feeling the intriguing Ariadne was just the woman to finally make this so.

She would come. He had no doubts about that. She was a smart woman, clearly, not jumping at the bait without thinking it through.

But she would not be able to resist the money. He'd done his homework on Ariadne Malis. She had managed to scrape together a living by boxing and working at the boxing gym—teaching mostly these days. But all her money went to caring for her mother. A woman who, by all accounts, liked drink and gambling more than she liked caring for her daughter.

Which made Ariadne's money situation even more fraught.

She would come. She would not be able to help herself. Zervou knew this with as much certainty as he had in him.

The only thing he did not know was if she was *aware* her father was such a despicable man. If she knew his identity at all.

He would find out tonight.

"Mr. Kritikos, your guest has arrived."

"Thank you, Bacchus. Bring her here and let the kitchens know I'd like our dinner to be served out here as well. It is a nice evening."

"Yes, sir."

Bacchus disappeared and in a few minutes returned with Ariadne.

She was dressed, he believed somewhat defiantly, in low, over-size cargo pants and heavy-soled boots paired with a formfitting black tank top. Her dark hair—wavy and interesting—was pulled back in a much more haphazard manner than it had been at the gym, so it spilled down her back, even if it was up away from her face. If she wore any makeup, it was done with a light hand. Freckles popped out across her nose next to a thin, gold hoop that matched the array of ones up the lobe of her ear.

She gave off a much different aura this evening. Casual. Young. Aside from the obvious musculature of her arms, and the slightly crooked bent of her nose, one might never guess she spent so much of her time trading punches.

Zervou had his choice of elegant, sophisticated, intelligent and beautiful women the world over. He'd chosen well, on more than one occasion, and enjoyed satisfying affairs with many of them.

It was a slight irritation that she was the first one to truly fascinate him in a long time.

"You don't live in Corfu," she said by way of greeting.

"How do you know?"

"I know who you are. And I would have heard if you lived here."

"I purchased this estate last week," he said, making a gesture to encompass the large balcony that stretched out over the town below. "It will not be my permanent address, but I'd like to keep a closer eye on the stadium as it is built."

"And this required buying an entire estate?"

"Fysiká."

She did not roll her eyes but somehow gave the impression of such. She made a production of looking around the terrace. A table was set up for dinner as the evening was nice, the breeze calm instead of irritating. Bacchus poured the wine and then disappeared inside. No doubt to signal to the rest of the waitstaff that they were ready for the first course.

"Come, Ms. Milas. Have a seat."

She stayed exactly where she was, though she crossed her arms over her chest. It caused the gap between the hem of her shirt and the waistband of her pants to widen and the little gold hoop at her belly button to sparkle in the low light of the terrace and the silvery illumination of the moon bouncing off the sea.

She was a beauty. It was impossible to deny. Interesting and sharp with it. She would stand out, no doubt. Even if he did not reveal her parentage, there would be talk of the new woman he had on his arm.

Once she agreed.

Which she would.

The waitstaff appeared, then paused when they realized no one was sitting. Zervou motioned for them to put the plates down on the table anyway. He watched as Ariadne followed the plates with her eyes.

There was greed in her gaze, but she still held herself back. Studying, assessing, no doubt looking for the dagger she seemed to think would come. But she was here.

So Zervou approached the table, pulled her chair out, but did not wait for her to sit. Instead, he took his own seat and made a bit of a show of shaking out his napkin and placing it over his knee.

Then he slipped the envelope of money out of his pocket and placed it at the center of the table. "Here is your payment."

He did not watch her as he chose what to put on his plate. His chef had put together a variety of appetizers, and Zervou planned to enjoy himself even if Ariadne spent the whole evening skulking about the edges of the shadows on the terrace.

"And what's to stop me from simply taking the money and running?" Ariadne asked after he'd filled his plate.

He glanced up at her. Took his time taking a bite of the *melitzana* before responding. "Nothing, of course."

She narrowed her eyes. "That's it? Nothing."

He lifted a negligent shoulder. “I told you I would pay you for coming to dinner. You came. So there is your money. If you are interested in more, then you will stay and eat. I have a proposition for you.”

Something in her expression darkened. “You wouldn’t be the first.”

He chuckled in spite of himself. She thought she knew who and what he was because of the fools she’d no doubt dealt with in her life. But she did not know Zervou Kritikos, clearly. “It does not involve sex.”

She eyed him a bit warily. Distrust but perhaps not full-on disbelief. “Then what does it involve?”

He had considered this part carefully. For a while, he’d even planned to romance her. Convince her it was all real. But that had felt a bit too much like leaving a victim in his wake. Zervou believed in revenge and retribution, but he did not believe in collateral damage. Not when he had been such.

So, he went with the truth. A direct kind of truth seemed to suit her anyway. It was its own kind of blow. Would she dodge it? Return her own? He couldn’t wait to find out.

“Your father.”

He watched as her entire body stilled with tension. She tried to remain relaxed on the outside, but something about the word *father* certainly surprised her. If they were boxing, he’d have landed a blow.

So he added the rest, a one-two punch, so to speak. “And revenge.”

Her chin came up. Her eyes flashing. Ready to deliver the return blow. He found himself smiling.

“I do not have a father,” she said flatly.

He tilted his head and considered her, the smile still on his face. He did love a spar. "Then I suppose the name Erjon Hyseni means nothing to you."

He could see it flash in her eyes. She knew. Which made his plan that much easier to implement.

He settled back in his chair, sipped his wine and knew he would enjoy this bout.

Ari had to bite her tongue to keep from demanding how he knew who her father was. He had to be in some kind of business with her father to know that because Erjon and her mother were the only ones who knew.

Weren't they? That had always been her understanding, but Ari knew that no matter what facts she managed to scrabble together, it was never the whole story. Never the whole truth.

Except one simple fact.

Her father was an evil man who had assaulted her mother. Who had made her childhood a violent jungle gym of threats and fear. Until ten years ago when he had disappeared, gone into hiding, leaving her only with the threat of his return someday.

That had given her time to build herself into the kind of machine who would deal with any threat.

But she hadn't seen this silk dagger coming—she could admit she'd expected some kind of sexual proposition. Or maybe something to do with boxing. She knew that most men saw that as the two things she had to offer.

Perhaps she should have known Zervou Kritikos would not follow *most*.

Any mention of her father should certainly send her running. She should grab the envelope and walk out, but the smell of dinner was wafting in the air, and she had not eaten much today. Mother had somehow convinced the grocer to give her alcohol in place of Ari's standing order of food for the week. It left her in a tight spot—not just financially but in terms of now needing to find a new grocer to make a deal with.

She hoped the sound of her stomach growling did not reach Zervou. *That* would be embarrassing, and whatever this was, however he knew about Erjon, to show any weakness to this man would be a death sentence. She didn't need to know anything to know that.

But was there any use denying the truth? Even if she didn't think he should know it. She wasn't worried about keeping the secret. Not in the way most people might. Because when she ended her father and his threats and the shadow he'd created over her and her mother's life, she would want everyone to know *why*.

"You see, Hyseni murdered my father, in cold blood," Zervou said, as if commenting on the weather. "In front of my mother. When I was just a boy."

For a moment, good sense warred with a soft heart. It was easy to think a man with his wealth and power had never suffered, but she knew better. Life was suffering.

And though she could not imagine the powerful man before her as anything so small and inconsequential as a boy, she could picture *a* child in that position. And she knew just how much children suffered.

"I am sorry to hear that," she said, wishing she did not sound quite so soft.

He paused in lifting another bite from his plate to his mouth. He looked at her as if she'd surprised him, though she didn't understand how or why. "Ever since that moment, I have vowed to find my revenge. I was close ten years ago, but he managed to escape my plans for him."

Ten years ago. Ari's breath caught. *This* man was responsible for her father being in hiding? It seemed… Well, she could see why someone would hide from him. He had a ruthless sharpness about him. It seemed he tried to mask it under wealth and prestige maybe, some easy charm, but there was no hiding a weapon.

Not from Ari.

Still, she didn't seem to have the good sense to fear him.

"He will not escape this time. And since I have spent the past decade learning everything there is to know about Erjon, I learned of your existence. I have spent years planning my retribution."

Join the club, she wanted to tell him. But even with a common enemy, she knew better than to trust a man such as Zervou Kritikos. Of course, that didn't mean she couldn't *use* a man such as he. If she was careful,

"I think you might just be the key, Ariadne Milas. Or should I say Ariadne Hyseni?"

"My name has never been Hyseni," Ari replied, trying to keep the snap out of her tone. Failing.

"My apologies."

He did not sound apologetic. Or trustworthy. Or safe. Still… She could at least get a decent meal and that envelope of cash out of this, couldn't she? Hesitantly, she moved toward the table, lowered herself into the chair. Everything smelled like heaven. Her stomach rumbled loudly.

She pretended she didn't hear it and filled her plate casually. Before she took the first bite though, she grabbed the envelope and shoved it deep into her pocket. She didn't need to count it. If he'd lied about the amount, she'd discover it after she left and react accordingly.

For now, she was getting a dinner out of…whatever this was. "How did you discover *my* connection?"

"My men unearthed a police report. A sexual assault. Against your mother. The timing was…in line with you being born."

Ari felt a roar in her ears, a heat in her face. Any hunger pangs she'd felt turned to a heavy weight of dread in her stomach. She tried not to freeze, but with her body a riot of negative reaction and her mind trying to make sense of his words, she no doubt looked like some kind of deer caught in headlights.

It had never occurred to her that her mother might have…actually reported it. It made it worse, somehow, that she had.

And no one had done anything.

But it changed nothing of what had happened, nothing of what she knew. So there was no reason for this… shame, this…whatever it was making her feel sick to her stomach.

"It seemed to me," Zervou continued. "That you, too, might have a taste for revenge against the man. So, I learned about you. And what a fascinating character I stumbled across. You are lethal, Ariadne."

She didn't feel very lethal right now, but she knew she needed to maintain that outer shell. She lifted her chin, met his gaze. "So are you, Zervou Kritikos. At least, you have the money to be."

His mouth curved, and she was not naive, so she

read the sharp blade of threat in that smile. He no doubt thought he'd hidden it behind charm and wealth.

But Ari knew every sharp blade was dangerous.

"So, I have developed a plan, as the one thing I have not been able to do is ferret your father out of whatever cave he hides himself in."

"Do not call him that," she snapped.

"What? A ferret? I can assure you—"

"My father. Do not call him my father."

"Ah. Noted."

Noted. She felt…foolish. Like a petulant child. But she *wasn't*. She forced herself to take a bite of food. Even though there was a glass of wine in front of her, she ignored it and took a sip of water to wash the food down through her too-tight throat. No doubt it was delicious, but she couldn't manage to taste it.

"My proposal is this. We will begin to be seen out together. Photographed. Let the whispers intimate that there is something going on between us. Then we will fake an engagement. Play it up in the papers. Draw your… Draw Erjon out. There is no way he will stand for his daughter being engaged to the man who sent him running in the first place. He will feel forced to act."

Ari sipped her water, studying the confident, too-handsome man before her.

She wasn't sure she agreed that Erjon would feel forced. It had potential, though. Erjon would certainly not want her marrying someone with the kind of wealth and power that could be stronger than his own threats and influence.

She also had long assumed his vague threats of return, of *using her for what she was worth*, involved selling her off to his cronies. Perhaps he'd already promised her to them—though they had not come to collect yet. Erjon had probably made it so they couldn't until he was free to reap the rewards.

He wouldn't want her making her own reward, that was for sure.

She eyed Zervou. Did the plan really make sense? Or was it a lie she was meant to fall for just because she wanted revenge? "Do you really think anyone will be all that interested in your choice of fiancée? Even if I am an unlikely choice."

He smiled at her, all sharp edges and ill-intent. "I always garner interest, *glikí mou*."

Well, that was probably true. Even if he didn't, he could likely pay to garner interest. But engaging in some kind of fake relationship seemed rather...silly, when besting Erjon was not a silly matter.

She had no doubt her father had done exactly what Zervou claimed. He was not above murder. She had never seen even a shred of humanity from the man. If he'd ever had any, his involvement as an enforcer for a crime family had certainly killed it.

But Erjon was...savvy. He might sniff it out as a trick from the start. He'd sniffed out all her other attempts to track him down and end the noose around her neck. And put one on his.

"And if we play up this engagement, and he remains in hiding?" Ari asked.

"You will have enjoyed all the benefits of being connected to me for a time—wealth, influence, et cetera. No harm. No foul."

Ari doubted it. There was always harm and foul when

you gambled. She had learned that one the hard way thanks to her mother. Perhaps this was not traditional gambling, but it was still a gamble.

Or was it…simply a risk? She took a risk every time she stepped in the ring. Every fight she agreed to. Every blow she didn't dodge was a risk. One she took on willingly. Because it made her feel alive.

Some of Zervou's staff appeared with a new array of plates of food. One person cleared the first round, while the other served them the new course.

Ari practically drooled. Not only was it food, and she was hungry, but it was good food. Fancy. No doubt Zervou engaged in only that which was fancy. But it wasn't… fussy. There was a heft to the food that left her feeling satisfied after she'd polished off her plate without saying anything else about his proposition.

And he did not force the conversation. He did not reiterate his plan. He let her eat in a companionable kind of silence.

"You do not like wine?" he asked casually, making it clear that even in silence, he was paying attention.

"I do not drink."

"Ah."

His *ah* spoke volumes. The kind of volumes that reminded her he'd done his research. If he'd discovered Erjon was her father, then he knew about her mother as well.

Dessert was served, something decadent and so chocolatey she could smell it over the fragrant jasmine that erupted out of pots on the perimeter of the patio.

Ari rose. As much as she desperately wanted to taste that chocolate confection, she knew when and how to make an exit mean something. "I'll think about this… proposition," she told Zervou. And she would. Carefully weigh both sides of this confusing situation and intriguing offer.

"You have not asked what your compensation would be," Zervou replied.

Ari didn't blink, though she wanted to. She'd assumed the revenge was the compensation, but she was enough of a businesswoman to not betray her ignorance. "I like to make sure I'm aligned with an opportunity before I discuss terms." She gave herself an internal pat on the back because, damn, that sounded good.

"Hmm. Well, interesting. Should you accept the proposal, come prepared with a list of demands."

Demands. It was hard to imagine this man accepting anyone's *demands*. "And you'll just capitulate to all of them?"

He laughed, low and dark, the sound a strange caress against her skin. Like a warm breeze that made goose bumps rise across her arms even though they shouldn't. "Of course not. We will negotiate."

Negotiate. It was a good word, and a good thing to remind herself she had leverage here. This was not a handout. It was not charity. It might not even be a trap.

It was a *business proposition.*

"Are you staying in Corfu?" she asked him, her eyes roaming the beautiful patio with its sparkling view. Had he really just bought this to keep an eye on his stadium being built? It seemed excessive. She supposed rich people could be excessive.

"For the foreseeable future. You have my card. Call

when you've reached your decision, and we will set up another meeting."

She nodded, expecting something more. A well-placed threat. Maybe even some kind of entreaty—not that she could imagine this man asking for anything. Though he had, hadn't he? Her cooperation. Of course, he'd somehow made it sound like a business deal, not any kind of favor or task he was asking her to do. No, if she agreed, they would work together to lure her father out of hiding.

And then Zervou would have his revenge—a revenge no doubt better than anything Ari could do outside of an actual fistfight.

All she risked was being in the orbit of a rich, powerful man who could squash her like a bug with both his influence and his wealth.

And you've been avoiding being squashed by the more powerful your whole life, haven't you?

She moved away from the table, toward the exit. She would think about it. Weigh the pros and cons. Consider her *demands*. She would not let herself be swayed by a delicious meal and manners.

"Oh and, Ariadne?"

She stopped at the door, bracing herself for some kind of parting shot. Some rug-pulling statement that would undo everything she'd just reluctantly started to believe in. Hope for.

"The deal is not *about* sex," he said, looking at her with dark, gleaming intent. "But it is hardly off the table if you should decide you're interested."

Ari didn't allow herself to react outwardly. She just

looked away and walked. Off the terrace, out of the sprawling house and then away from the luxurious estate.

But the little bolt of heat that seared through her midsection was a bit of a concerning problem.

CHAPTER THREE

ZERVOU WAS A patient man—when patience was warranted. He also knew how to press an advantage. After Ariadne had left, he'd instructed his staff to wrap up the dessert and deliver it to her apartment. She would not know what to do with that.

He appreciated her wariness, even if it was in opposition to what he was trying to accomplish. He understood her reticence, and no amount of perks was going to allow her to let down her guard.

He had no doubt she'd eventually agree. It was too good of a deal—he could afford to offer her too much for her to refuse. Her life beyond her boxing successes seemed rather sad.

Yes, he was offering her too much to refuse, but he respected the way she'd handled herself in spite of that. The way she was handling this. With a carefulness and a confidence.

Yes, he liked what made up Ariadne Malis.

And, over the next two days, he often found himself thinking far too often of the way the gold of her belly button ring had sparkled in the moonlight, there against smooth skin over hard muscle.

He wanted to see her box again. He wanted to see her

to do many things. And while many around him might consider him a man who did not do without what he wanted, internally Zervou was a much more measured and careful man.

He did not allow himself wants if they did not fit into the plans he had for his life. Now, he had the power and influence to make most of his wants fit into those plans, but retribution was one exception.

So a fascinatingly complex attraction to the woman he needed to draw out his sworn enemy was something to be carefully assessed, considered. It required treading lightly.

But, as he'd told her, sex was hardly off the table if she was interested.

For the time being, he needed to continue preparations. He assumed Ariadne would make him wait. His guess was she would come to him with agreement in a week. He didn't love patience, but he was considering Ariadne a kind of partner in this. He wanted her willing and ready and thinking more was in her control than actually was.

He believed this was a tactical necessity. He had no doubt her demands would be negligible to someone like him. Some money. Some assurances. She likely couldn't imagine more than a drop in the hat of what he'd accrued.

So he prepared for what would happen when she finally capitulated. He already had people working on a wardrobe for her—though he liked the tough-girl casual that clearly suited her, it would not suit the events they would be going to. He already had his social assistant working on accepting invitations to all the most important parties around Europe and the travel required. Organizing the press they would need to make sure Erjon would hear of their relationship no matter what kind of hole the man had dug himself into.

Though Zervou had not been able to sniff out any yet, he had no doubt there was some kind of tabs being kept on Ariadne from the Hyseni camp. Erjon would know what his daughter was up to. And he would be forced to act.

Zervou could see no other way this went.

So he could be patient for a few more days. He could wait for Ariadne to come to him. He could wait for everything to work out just the way he planned.

A knock sounded at his office door before it moved open and Bacchus stepped inside. "Mr. Kritikos. We have a…situation. With Ms. Malis."

Zervou frowned. He thought she'd make him wait at least three days minimum. "Is she here?"

"No. But we were watching the apartment and her mother as you suggested. Based on my investigation, Maria Malis has racked up quite a debt with the Sakkas family. Their toughs plan to collect this evening. It is… unlikely Maria or Ariadne have the funds to pay."

"I see."

It did not look like they were going to be able to wait for Ariadne to come to the correct conclusions herself. "Get the required cash. We will handle this."

"Yes, sir. Would you like me to pay off the Sakkas family or give the money directly to Ms. Malis?"

Zervou considered his options.

"I'd like to handle this one myself. Ready the car and the payoff. I will be down momentarily."

* * *

Ari jogged up the stairs to her apartment. Her muscles screamed in protest but keeping them moving after a tough training session was better than babying them. At least in the long run.

Her lip throbbed from where she'd gotten a punch because she'd been busy thinking about her life, about the piece of chocolate cake Zervou had sent over, and not enough about her practice.

So she had to make a decision tonight. One way or another. Even if she ended up flipping a coin. The decision had to be made before tomorrow's training. Once made, it couldn't distract her. She wouldn't let it.

And how could she refuse? Sure, Zervou had the kind of power to ruin her life if she made a wrong move, but how could she turn her back on the chance to ruin her father just to survive a few more days in this dog-eat-dog world? If Zervou ruined her, did it matter if they ruined Erjon first?

Your mother needs you.

The point she kept circling back to. Sure, she had plenty to risk—there was no magical future she hoped for. Just survival, really, and even that seemed...negligible. Except if anything happened to her—if she lost her ability to fight, to work, anything like that—her mother would end up destitute and homeless. Or worse.

Probably much worse. Ari shook her head, reaching into her bag for her keys as she approached the apartment door.

"Ariadne Malis."

Ari nearly jumped at the unfamiliar voice saying her name. She didn't hide it well, either. She really had to get out of her own head. She was putting herself in danger, and that didn't work in her world.

She turned to face two men, put her back to her apartment door. For a split second, she thought maybe they were another pair of men sent by Zervou, but a quick survey of the wardrobe ruled that out. These men were dressed with flash over any kind of substance. It screamed wanting to look rich without actually *being* rich.

Which wasn't good. Dread pooled in her gut.

She didn't let the dread show. "Can I help you gentlemen?"

"I don't suppose you're aware of where your mother has been spending her evenings."

Really not good. "She likes to knit," Ari replied with a saccharine smile. This would not be the first time her mother's…habits had brought rough men to their door making demands. Ari knew how to handle the muscle sent to shake down poor women with gambling problems.

"You must be confused," the man said, meeting her fake sweetness with a fake politeness of his own. "Maria Malis spends her time in the Sakkas Casino. Losing more money than she has to lose at our tables."

Ari swore inwardly but maintained the smile. Sakkas Casino wasn't her mother's usual fare of laying a few wages on horses or the numbers she liked to pick in the back room of the grocery. Sakkas was…serious. And there would be serious consequences for not repaying such a debt.

Damn. Ari had to think fast. She lifted a shoulder to the man's accusation. She stealthily moved her hand to the knob, hoping Mom had left the door unlocked even though Ari always reminded her to lock it if she left.

It turned in her hand. *Hallelujah.* Getting inside wouldn't save her when one man had a gun, but it would buy some time. She just needed some time to plan.

"Sounds like a you problem," she told the men, holding the knob so she could pull it open and slip in before they had a chance to—

One slammed his hand against the door before she could get it open. "You'd be wrong." He looked down at her. Eyes hard and mean. "It's a *you* problem now."

Ari eyed the two men hulking over her. She could probably take them. With the right strategy, with the right moves.

Unfortunately, she couldn't exactly fight off a gun. Unless she managed to land a hard enough blow that the one with the gun fell back and down the stairs. If that worked, she could immediately whirl and likely duck a grab made by the second man. But he could have another kind of weapon. Maybe a knife.

Of course, she had one of those, too. But she'd have to get it *while* taking out the one with the gun.

"Seems to me all those boxing prizes come with a bit of money. The kind of money that might go a ways toward paying off a debt." This came from the one with the gun.

She didn't need to tell him he couldn't be more wrong. He wouldn't believe her anyway. Still, she thought of the money Zervou had handed over the night before last. She'd bought groceries with some of it and secreted the rest away. She *could* offer it as a start of payment…

But where did it end? *Don't worry about the end. Just get through this day. One step at a time.*

"Listen—"

A strange…tsking noise sounded behind them. Both men looked over their shoulders, but Ari could not see what was there around the two large men. Still, she could use this surprise to her advantage. If she started a fight, she could get inside. Grab the money. Grab Mom. And run.

Run where?

Anywhere, really. Anywhere was better than this.

She was about to deliver the first blow when a voice surprised her.

"Surely violence isn't necessary."

Surely that wasn't… But as the two men adjusted their stances, she caught sight of him.

Zervou.

He was dressed just as he had been when they'd dined together. A suit that could not be mistaken for anything but the best of the best, made expressly to fit his broad shoulders. Subtle, sophisticated, perfect.

He oozed all of those things while standing on the grimy landing in front of her dilapidated apartment door. While two-bit enforcers stood there in their cheap suits and overwhelming cologne thinking they were important because they'd taken advantage of a drunk woman's weakness for cards.

"This isn't any of your business," the man with the gun said. He put his hand in his jacket, clearly showing the gun off to Zervou.

Who did not so much as flinch. Instead, he produced

a big, fat envelope. “This should more than take care of the debt.”

Ari swallowed. She should protest. She’d be even more indebted to him if she allowed him to pay off her mother’s debts, but… It would buy some time. She could figure this out with a reprieve.

The man who wasn’t armed reached out to snatch the envelope of cash, but Zervou must have held fast, creating what would have looked like some kind of foolish tug of war if Zervou were anyone else.

Instead, he looked down at the man with cold, direct eyes, power emanating from him like a visible entity. “You will not come back here.”

The man tugged on the envelope again, but it didn’t come free. “If there are no more debts—”

“You misunderstand me. Do not extend credit to people who cannot pay, and there will be no more debts. You will not come back here. If you do, the Sakkos family will have a very formidable enemy. I don’t think either of us wants that.”

The man with the gun snorted. “Listen—”

“Oh no, my friend. It is you who will listen. And I suggest you run it by your bosses before you decide to make an enemy out of Zervou Kritikos.”

The name seemed to shock both men. They exchanged a look. One cleared his throat. The other spoke. Deferentially at that.

“Understood, Mr. Kritikos.”

Zervou finally let go of the envelope, and the two men skittered off like Zervou had invoked some kind of potential curse upon them.

Should she be concerned that his name spoken to the

toughs of Corfu could be invoked like a curse? *Yes. Obviously.*

He stood there like something as threatening as a curse. His expression vaguely amused as he studied her there, leaning against her door.

She could only stare at him as her heart rate slowly returned to normal. As the adrenaline that had rushed through her started to fade. Suddenly she was just tired. Bone-deep weary.

"Do you always carry a wad of cash around?" she asked. "I wouldn't recommend it in this neighborhood, even with your fancy security detail."

He said nothing to this, and everything inside of her deflated. No, he didn't carry cash around. Of course not. His arrival wasn't happenstance or him coming to talk more about his proposition. It was a plan.

He'd known. "You knew."

He said nothing still, but it was clear. He'd somehow known these men had come to shake her down. And he'd come with the money because that would mean she would owe him. She would have to take his deal, whether she wanted to or not.

She should have known it was all an act. This idea she had choice. "I suppose I'm indebted to you now."

"It appears that way." He moved closer, his eyes on her face, narrowed. Studying her with such an intensity she found herself holding her breath with every step closer he took. His mouth curved down into a frown. "You have a split lip." His thumb brushed gently just under where her lip throbbed, causing a new kind of throb to begin low in her stomach.

It took her a moment to breathe through the bolt of

heat, this strange vibrating inside of her. She had to be made of tougher stuff than melting at a man's unwanted touch.

Is unwanted the word you're looking for here?

"It wasn't from them," she said, ignoring her traitorous thoughts. "Bumps and bruises are part of my job."

He made a considering sound, while his thumb lingered there at the corner of her mouth. Gentle.

Erotic.

She tried to focus on the pain from her practice rather than the unraveling pleasure in him standing this close, looking at her that intently, touching her no matter how innocently.

Innocent? Zervou?

Yeah, definitely not the right word. But she was a fighter. She wouldn't take these blows without some of her own.

"I have demands." She lifted her chin. She knew how to fight even when she lacked every advantage. She knew how to pretend there was anything left in the tank, even when there wasn't. Because right now, what she really wanted to do was curl up in her bed and cry.

Too bad.

He held her gaze. She could read nothing in his expression. But when he spoke, there was a strange softness in his tone that she could not categorize.

"Then let us go inside and hash them out."

CHAPTER FOUR

ZERVOU COULD READ the reluctance in her, even as she turned to open her apartment door. Even with his body tight and his skin humming with all that *want* he'd told himself to control.

He did not like the sight of her lip puffy and bloody. It had twisted inside of him sharp and foreign. But it had eased something to know it was a blow she'd taken voluntarily instead of scrabbling with those hulking men and their pathetic threats.

It had eased something to touch her, to feel the way she stilled under his touch, her breath caught, her eyes wide.

Yes, he liked catching Ariadne a little off guard.

But that feeling didn't last as he followed her into her apartment. It was neat enough, but everything sagged with the weight of poverty. Cramped, clearly. The vague scent of alcohol seemed to permeate every air molecule.

It reminded him of the places his mother had insisted on living, though it had never been *her* drinking. No, his mother preferred to take on the role of saint. Refuse any and all help—even his money and his help once he'd garnered the ability to offer both. So married to her pride. Her suffering. Nothing had mattered except that.

Certainly not him.

It was only when his grandmother had begun to suffer from dementia that his mother had allowed him to help at all. For her mother. Never for herself.

Never for him.

Now they lived with a nurse in a nicer cottage in the hometown he wanted nothing to do with.

He did not wish to think of such things, did not like the way they dissolved everything he'd felt out on that landing. He even considered whisking Ariadne away to his estate so they could have a discussion of terms without memories assaulting him.

But he was made of stronger stuff, and this setting only proved his point and how much she could use his offer.

There was a small table in the kitchen just steps away from the door, so he moved toward it. Took a seat.

Ariadne eyed him warily, still standing by the door. "I have to check on my mother. I'll be right back." She disappeared down the hall and then returned a few minutes later without the bag she'd been carrying. She offered nothing about the state of her mother.

She did not take the seat opposite him. Instead she rested a hip against the kitchen counter, arms crossed over her chest, expression hard and defiant.

Because he wanted to move this along so he could be out of here, he didn't wait for her to start. "Before we get to your demands, I have a few of my own to make clear. For example, your mother. I cannot have her creating… problems while we do this. Something must be done to get her out of the way, out of trouble."

Ariadne's expression didn't so much as flicker. "Good luck there."

The bitterness in her tone did not surprise him, but the way it echoed inside of him did. The understanding of being shackled to someone you wanted to help, who refused such help. Over and over again.

But this was not the same. His mother was stubborn. Her mother was addicted—an illness. Not a choice.

"There are centers for these kinds of things. These addictions."

"Yes, and they cost money. You also tend to have to be a willing participant for any of those centers to matter."

"I will foot the bill, of course. You'll have your pick of the best facilities in Greece."

Ariadne blinked at that, her shoulders sagging a little. "My…pick," she repeated, as if she did not understand the words.

"Yes. Whichever facility you want. I will get in her in, and I will pay her way. Perhaps it works. Perhaps it doesn't. This is irrelevant to me so long as she stays there while we draw Erjon out."

She said nothing. He waited, and still she simply stood there. He was a patient man, but she was testing it. Or maybe the cracks in the table in front of him were testing it.

"I seem to recall you saying you had demands," he told her, looking away from the cracks. The only part of this place that did not remind him of all he'd pulled himself out of was her.

"I want it to be clear that I do not trust things that sound too good to be true," she said fiercely. "I do not trust windfalls."

Which were not demands at all.

"You do not need to trust anything," Zervou replied, watching the anger in her expression. Why were women so bound and determined to be angry when he offered to take care of things? It should be met with gratitude, but he always seemed to find himself faced with stubborn, pointless *pride*.

Frustration simmered within him, but he did not let it take hold. He kept his seat and his tone neutral. "You only need to do as you're told."

She stiffened, and he found himself reliving the feel of her skin under his thumb. The catch of her breath and that flash of heat in her eyes before she'd blinked it away. Because she reacted to the words *do what you're told* in much the same way.

Physical reaction. Which stirred one of his own.

"I don't generally do that, either," she said after a moment, never quite meeting his gaze.

Fascinating. "Well, some sacrifices must be made to get what we want."

"We." Bitter again. So used to being on her own, he supposed. He knew a bit about that, didn't he? And trying to save those who did not wish to be saved. And all these similarities had one root cause.

"Erjon Hyseni will pay. That is what you want, is it not?"

She stared straight ahead at the wall. Her voice was devoid of any emotion, but her expression was fierce. "Yes, that is what I want."

"Then it is a *we*, *glikí mou*. You do not need to trust me. Use me." He smiled when she looked over at him. "And I shall use you."

Ari felt…unsettled. Unmoored. The way he said things did something to her. Internally. Chemically. She was not used to feeling like someone else was in the driver's seat of her body's reaction.

She knew how to take blows, how to land them. She did not know what to do with *him*.

"What are your demands then? I have already paid off your mother's debt. I will foot the bill for your mother's recovery. You will also be given an allowance. Money is no object here, Ariadne."

"An allowance? Like a child?" Why she was being petulant she didn't know, except she needed to find some clear, grounded footing, and fighting always did that for her.

"We could call it a…weekly salary if you prefer," he said, so unoffended, so easy. "You will be paid for your time. Enacting your duties."

"Which are?"

"Your duties will be everything required to play your role. To appear as my companion, then fiancée. To attend whatever dinners, parties, events I require. To have your picture taken, to be interviewed—this will require some media training, of course."

"And what of boxing?"

"You may continue through your next bout. Ideally, Erjon has crawled his way out of whatever sewer he finds himself in by then. If not, you may have to take a break from organized fights, though you will still be able to train if you wish. If we should have to get married—"

"*Kratitheíte*, married?" This was insanity. Marriage was…legally binding. She had no romantic notions about the institution, but it still spoke of partnership and intimacy and trust—even a marriage based on pretense. There was legality and risk—to her, the party with nothing.

Why was she even considering this ordeal? Did she really think he'd let her have access to all this money? All these…options. When she'd never had any. Just to… play pretend?

"If it need go that far, you will be compensated even more generously in a divorce settlement."

It was all too good to be true. It couldn't possibly work out this way. He had to be lying, tricking her. He certainly would have no reason to keep his word on this.

But the money he'd given the Sakkos enforcers was no trick. It could come with strings that were tricks, but the debt was paid either way. Mom would be safe for at least a little while—which was more than Ari could do herself.

Could she say no, if the debts were paid either way?

She could deny the answer for a few more days. Convince herself there was another way. But there wasn't. There never was.

And if it brought Erjon out of hiding… If this rich and powerful man enacted revenge against the man she wanted to be free of…

Wasn't it worth any cost?

Mom passed out in her room made that clear, didn't it?

She lifted her chin, met his gaze. She was a fighter. What was this but another fight? Another bout? She could do it. And if she didn't get all the prize he offered, at least she'd get some.

"When do I start?"

His mouth curved, danger and something that affected her body on some unknown cellular level glittered in his eyes. Her brain knew better than to trust this man, but it was as if there was some unknown force inside her overriding what her usually smart mind could determine.

"Tomorrow. I will pick you up for dinner. Be expecting a package in the morning with your required wardrobe."

"I don't love the word *required*."

He rose. He moved for the door, but that required him to brush past her in the tiny kitchen. He smelled like something faintly woodsy, no doubt an unimaginably expensive cologne.

He met her gaze, dark and intent. "Get used to it," he said firmly before letting himself out the door.

Ari stood where she was, breathing through the effect this man had on her. Breathing through this…insanity she was agreeing to.

When the wardrobe came the next morning, along with information about a few rehabilitation centers in Greece—all of them luxurious, expensive and very private—Ari knew she was in trouble. But if this trouble came with her parents getting what they deserved—her mother help, her father punishment—then Ari would make whatever sacrifices, pay whatever costs.

No matter what.

CHAPTER FIVE

ZERVOU INSTRUCTED HIS DRIVER to park outside Ariadne's apartment complex and then retrieve her, while Zervou waited in the car.

While he wanted to lure Erjon out of hiding, he knew he had to be careful. Two sightings in this—well, *slum* was really the only word for it—within two days would be suspicious, but if it seemed like he was trying to hide his identity the second day…

Yes, that worked better for his purposes. Though he hated to give Erjon any credit, he'd been hunting the man for years to no avail. There was some intelligence in the man to be able to stay out of Zervou's reach.

When his driver returned, Ariadne following behind him, Zervou watched. She had dressed in what he'd sent over this morning. Admittedly, he'd half expected her to be defiant for defiance's sake and refuse.

But she wore the high-necked dress that went all the way down to the ground, hugging the lines of her body beautifully. Her arms were bare. Her hair was down in a riot of waves. If she wore makeup, it was minimal. A touch of color at her lips if that.

She looked dangerous in black. The musculature of her bare arms added to that danger, while the delicate gold rings she wore on her fingers and the band of dainty jewels around her wrist were the perfect hint of something softer, more elegant than the skilled brawler she was.

Perhaps the only nod to her own style was her usual hoops in her ears and nose and the shoes, which he only noticed as she was helped into the back seat—sneakers instead of the expensive sandals he'd supplied for her.

Since she somehow seemed to make it work, he didn't nitpick. It lent an aura of credibility to the whole thing if she didn't simply change overnight. "You look beautiful."

She eyed him warily as she settled into the seat next to him. "I feel a bit ridiculous. Dresses and jewels aren't my norm." She held up her wrist and let the bracelets jangle against each other as if proving her point.

"They are now, for the time being."

She made a vague kind of noise, no doubt meant to convey agreement without actually agreeing. She shifted in her seat, as if the luxurious limousine was somehow uncomfortable.

"Do you travel like this everywhere?" she asked, a hint of derision or disapproval in her tone.

"I travel in whatever ways I wish," he returned, a little bolt of irritation surprising him. He'd long ago learned how to move through life without letting irritation eat him from the inside out. He had built himself into a man who did not have to deal with irritations or frustrations or annoying people. He studied Ariadne with some curiosity. He supposed she might be the exception. As Erjon's daughter, he needed her—no matter how she behaved.

What a strange feeling.

"So, what exactly is the point of this dinner?"

"To be seen. Gossip is practically currency in the circles I walk among. We want all the rich and powerful in high society to want to know who my date is. The more the information permeates, the more it trickles down to the type of people Erjon associates with."

She seemed to consider this, but her eyebrows remained beetled together, the faint hint of a frown tugging the corners of her lips down. Like she was confused.

"You may be required to smile at me, once or twice," he offered. "A laugh or two wouldn't go astray." He reached out, skimmed a finger over the curve of her shoulder. He wasn't surprised that she jerked at the touch. It was kind of the point. "And a touch cannot cause you to jump a foot," he informed her.

She scowled. "I wasn't expecting it. I'm used to punching in response to unannounced touches." She laid this down as a bit of a challenge.

He couldn't help but be amused. "You will have to get used to keeping those fists unclenched while we are together." He placed his hand over hers—currently clenched in said fist. "Relax, Ariadne. There is no boxing match here. It is a meal. A bit of a performance."

Her hand didn't relax. She remained stiff next to him, her fingers clenched. Still, he left his hand atop the fist. There was something fascinating about the way tension coiled there, knowing she could do some damage if she'd like.

He ran his index finger along the bumps of her knuckles. Power changed to tension, to bracing. She was a myriad of reactions.

"Have you decided which facility you would like your mother to go to?" he asked, keeping his hand over hers.

She did not pull away, but she didn't relax into the casual touch, either. She took a careful breath before she spoke. "The one in Mykonos felt like the best fit, but—"

"Excellent choice," he replied over her excuses or objections or whatever was meant to come after the *but*. "I will make the arrangements, and then we shall take a trip to drop her off."

She eyed him. Would that wariness always poke at his temper? "We?" she demanded.

"Have you ever been to Mykonos?" he returned, keeping his voice casual. No one made him lose his temper anymore.

She looked ahead, a strange expression on her face he couldn't quite decipher. "No, I have never been anywhere," she said flatly.

"Well, that is about to change. You and I are about to see Europe together, *glikí mou*."

She frowned at him—not the usual response to finding out you had just earned yourself some all-expenses paid holidays. He convinced himself she simply didn't trust him to deliver. Once he did, all her reticence would leave, since that was what good sense dictated. She'd survived this long. She must have *some* sense.

"Do you have some objection to seeing Europe?"

"Of course not. I just… I do not know how to relax and trust this," she told him earnestly. A kind of earnestness that felt too…naked. A softness that would be crushed by all the world had to offer.

But no doubt Ariadne had already been crushed in a myriad of ways.

"Perhaps you should endeavor to try," he told her.

This did not change the soft confusion on her face,

even as the car pulled to a stop, and he got out. He skirted the car himself and opened the door for her.

He helped her out of the car, tucked her arm into his, turned to face the elegant restaurant. “Enjoy yourself, Ariadne,” he said, gesturing at the building in front of them. “Pain and suffering will no doubt come soon enough. Why not enjoy the respite while it’s here?”

Ari chewed over Zervou’s words the entire dinner. *Enjoy yourself.* Had she ever had such a luxury?

She’d certainly never had a meal in any place nearly this fancy. The tablecloths were a crisp white, the candlelight gave everything a romantic glow. The silverware gleamed like it was polished in between every use. Fresh flowers unfurled in a vase in the middle of the table in pretty pastels.

Everything felt gilt and wasteful almost, but it wasn’t…overstated. The feeling of waste came from her own life of scraping by for the bare minimum.

And in two days she would go to Mykonos. He’d mentioned *Europe.*

She had never been any of these places, not because there hadn’t been opportunities. Her skill in the boxing ring had garnered her many an offer. Athens. Bulgaria. A bout in Poland.

But she’d never been able to commit to leaving her mother, even if she would have been able to raise money to cover her travel expenses. So she only took local fights.

Perhaps with her mother in a facility, she could take on some upcoming fights outside of Corfu. Zervou had said he’d let her continue to box.

Enjoy yourself.

Mother would need to be settled. Happy, or whatever Maria's approximation of happy could be. Hopefully.

What would it look like to allow herself to enjoy this little windfall, knowing the rug would be pulled out from under her once her father was taken care of? Would it really be such a risk? Or would it simply be…a rest?

Bodies, muscles, reflexes required rest to grow stronger. Perhaps this would allow her the same. She had felt lately that she'd been failing her mother on a larger scale than ever before. Maybe this…break would allow her to fortify herself to do better.

The meal itself was exquisite. Even Zervou's company wasn't terrible. He was arrogant but not…pompous. With his buildings venturing into sporting arenas, they had some common ground on which to talk—at least, common ground that did not involve her father being the root of both their problems.

"Tell me, how does a young girl find herself in a boxing gym?" he asked after ordering dessert from the waiter.

Ari did not know how she could eat another bite but was tempted all the same. His question was less tempting.

She did not often get into full truths. They felt dangerous, like hints at ways to hurt her. But since it all revolved around the man they were working together to destroy, she felt the truth was better served here.

Still, she did not know where to begin. Boxing stemmed from something more than being physically capable. It was a seed planted by her father. Perhaps the only one that had ever borne fruit.

"My father was a kind of…specter growing up. He

wasn't always there, but the threat of him was. Sometimes he would appear at my school, walk me home and tell me he had plans for me. I was not always afraid of him. He seemed no more dangerous than my mother when she was drinking. But as I got older, I started to understand who he was, what he'd done and that no plan he had for me would be anything I wanted."

She could remember when she'd gone from a girl curious about the grumpy man who showed up from time to time claiming her as his, to a teenage girl who understood what her mother spoke of when she said Erjon had forced himself on her.

"I became angry. Always so…angry." *Perhaps you should not play victim then*, her father had once told her when she'd told him to leave her and her mother alone. With absolutely no way to back it up.

"At home I had to be good, or Mother would…fall off the wagon—alcohol, bets we couldn't afford, both." Erjon showing up to make demands and threats, speaking of his looming *plans* that even then Ari didn't have to know the details of to know they were bad. "But at school, I could not rein in my anger. I got in fights. I was a bully. Angry, violent."

"Desperate," Zervou said.

For a moment, she could only stare at him. It was an apt word. Too apt of a word. She didn't like him having any words to describe what she'd felt—uncontrollable and confusing to her young mind. She didn't like now having that word in her head. It was better, easier to think of it as anger.

She swallowed down the strange swell of emotion,

shoved it away where all the unwanted ones went, and went on with her story.

"A kind teacher who saw…something in me, I suppose, introduced me to a youth program at the boxing gym. It was only boys, but she did some fast talking to get me in. She must have paid for it, something I also didn't realize until later."

"Survival doesn't always allow us to realize everything going on around us."

Because his easy understanding or vindication or whatever this was felt like a stab to the gut, she went on the offensive. Her tone was cutting, disbelieving. "*You* have experienced survival?"

His mouth curved, but it was not anything so soft as a smile. It was a parry, if anything. "Life was not easy after my father was murdered. My mother would take no help."

"Ironic. My mother would have taken help, but my father ensured no one offered it." Her own countermove, because did he think he had somehow suffered when at least there had *been* help?

He said nothing to that, just watched her with intense dark eyes, like if he kept watching her long enough he would know all her secrets, upend all her foundations.

She would fight tooth and nail for that to never happen, which she supposed was why she ended up being more honest than she usually was. Without secrets, he could not upend her.

"I excelled in the boxing ring," she continued. "I beat all the boys, easily. I had all that anger inside me, and with instruction I could hone it. I liked the feeling of… turning it into a weapon. Controlling this thing inside me. It felt powerful. To choose how to land a blow. To accept my own. It felt like a tool I could use against him."

"Erjon?"

"Yes. He took an interest in my progress, but this was nearing the time when he disappeared. Before he left, he came to see me. He told me that when he was able to return, I would take my rightful place in his world. He did not come out and say it, but I believe he wanted to sell me off to one of his brainless crime lord bosses. Perhaps he already had." Ari lifted a shoulder. "But his disappearance was the one stroke of luck I have been given in my life, I suppose. For the first two years, I dreaded his return. But that seemed to give this…specter all the power, and when I turned eighteen and realized I was an adult, in charge, so to speak, I decided I would not dread it. I would prepare for it. He would not ruin me without a fight."

"You wanted him to come."

"Yes," she agreed. "There came a point when I did not want to wait. To let him choose the timing. I could not do anything to find him, but I hoped with enough success in the boxing ring I might draw him out. He wouldn't be able to resist putting me in my place. And when that occurred, instead of him coming through with whatever threats, I would end him."

Zervou raised one elegant brow. "End?"

"He ruined my mother's life. Everything she does is to cope with what he did to her. Everything I do is to keep her safe. Whatever ways I can end him, I will. It is the only reason I am here with you."

Zervou smiled at this, and she turned her attention to

the slice of dark chocolate mousse cake on her plate. She ate instead of deal with the effects of that smile.

"We are not so different, Ariadne," he said, his voice seeming…deeper, and far more dangerous. "I daresay we are quite alike."

The thought was insulting enough she looked back up at him. She eyed him, trying not to let bitterness win. But it was hard. He was sitting there in his fancy suit, and she was wearing clothes he'd bought. He had a plan to ensure her father rotted in jail forever that he could endlessly work toward and fund, while she had to work herself to the bone every day balancing keeping her mother safe and just hoping her notoriety in Corfu might draw Erjon out.

Whatever similarities they had, they were not the *same*.

He had been allowed some sort of luck or fruition or what have you to allow his hard work to turn into riches, beyond most people's wildest dreams. She was still scrabbling.

She could not blame him for this. The world was set up to reward men and punish women. That was all she'd ever seen. If it had been the other way around, she certainly would have accepted the world's rewards.

Still, she could not swallow down the bitterness enough to agree with him. So she ignored his statement and finished her dessert.

They walked out of the restaurant, her hand in his, their fingers entwined. A strange intimacy with a man she barely knew.

Except it was acting. A role she was playing. Not so different from how she moved through the world usually—

with a layer, a mask of armor. This was just a different kind. Instead of toughness, she had to appear…connected to someone.

Admittedly, she was struggling to know what that looked like enough to act it out.

But Zervou seemed to know. He led her outside and to his limousine. He opened the back door for her, but before he let her go to slide into the seat, he lifted her hand to his mouth.

He brushed his lips across her knuckles, the contact featherlight but somehow like an arrow. Sharp and piercing through the very center of her. A kind of yearning she associated with being hungry…pain and want intertwining with frustration of needs not met.

Her gaze flicked to his. That smug smile on his face.

He understood he was having an effect on her, physically at least. Which was infuriating in a way she didn't know what to do about. How did you fight someone like this?

You are a fighter, Ari. You will figure it out.

You have to.

CHAPTER SIX

As THEY DROVE back to Ariadne's apartment, Zervou considered the dinner quite the success. Not only had he gotten some background into Ariadne and her father's mark on her life—something that assured him his plan would work—but he'd also noticed some curious gazes from the people in the restaurant. No doubt whispers would start regarding him and his new dinner companion.

Everything was going according to plan. He only needed one more thing tonight. When they arrived at her apartment building, he pushed open his door.

"You are not coming up," Ariadne said. He would almost call it something like panic in her tone. An interesting concept. This woman who could defend herself in just about every physical way possible was...panicked at the idea of him going up to her apartment?

Yes, there were still depths to mine when it came to Ariadne Malis.

He raised an eyebrow at her. "Did you fancy yourself in charge?"

She frowned at him. "It is best if my mother doesn't interact with you until I can ensure she understands what's happening."

Zervou got to his feet and closed his door, moving

around the back of the vehicle so he could open hers. She had not waited for him, but she had not managed to get out of the seat yet.

"I do not need to engage with your mother," Zervou said, holding out his hand for her to take. "The whispers will have started. I can hardly drop you off at the curb, Ariadne. At the very least, you must allow me to behave a gentleman and walk you to your door."

"I do not think anyone in this neighborhood moves in the same circles as *you* for you to worry about anyone seeing such a thing," she replied, though she gingerly placed her hand in his and allowed him to help her out of the car.

"You would be surprised, Ariadne, just how much interest you garner and how even whispers that start here could reach people who want to be reached by them." He walked with her up the stairs to her apartment door. "Even now, someone could be watching."

She snorted inelegantly. "Yes, someone who wishes to relieve you of your wallet and phone."

Zervou did not bother to argue with her. She was not used to moving through the world with eyes on her at the level he was. Someone would be watching. Someone would mention it to someone and so on.

By tomorrow morning, the interest in Ariadne Malis, excellent boxer, would be piqued. He would no doubt have people calling him, suddenly wanting to invite him to even more dinners, events. All so they could maybe ask a question or catch a glimpse that might allow them to be the first to know why Zervou Kritikos would be seen in the same orbit as a female boxer from the absolute wrong neighborhood.

Besides, he had no doubt Erjon's minions would be the type to skulk about this neighborhood. But he did not want to point that out to Ariadne if she did not already know it.

They reached her door, and she quickly retrieved her keys from her purse, extricated herself from his hold and moved to unlock the door.

"Ariadne."

Her shoulders stiffened, and he watched as she very purposefully rolled them into relaxing. She turned to face him, chin lifted.

Fists clenched. Always ready to fight. He did not know why he found that so enticing. He would have thought he'd had enough fighting in his life. Her, too.

But here he was, fascinated, intrigued, wanting to know just how far it would take to snap that careful control of hers. Because she was always ready to fight, but she also held it in check.

So he stepped forward, because he would have to find a way under her natural propensities if they were to succeed in their mission. "Whether you like it or not, you have agreed to something. And that means behaving."

Temper sparked in her eyes, but she did not snap back. "And how should I behave?"

He moved in even closer, even as she pressed her back against her apartment door. He lowered his mouth to be close to her ear, so he could whisper the rest in case someone *was* watching.

And because he liked watching the way her breathing went unsteady.

"As though you are romantically interested, naturally.

Now, I am going to kiss you goodnight, and I must warn you, you cannot get any…ideas."

"Ideas?" She was trying to sound tough, but her voice had gone husky.

He bit back a smile. "Yes, the women I kiss tend to get ideas. Love, marriage, a future. These are not things I plan on offering anyone."

She huffed out a derisive sound. "Perhaps you are not nearly as charming as you give yourself credit for."

He lifted a negligent shoulder. "Perhaps," he agreed verbally…but did not agree internally, because he could see the effect he had on her.

Perhaps there was a glimmer of concern about the effect she had on him, but he could control things such as that.

He skimmed the back of his fingers along her jawline. She stood very still, though her jaw clenched. She did not betray any reaction, but he could see how hard she was working at betraying nothing.

It made him smile. And lean in.

"Why be worried, *glikí mou*?" he said, close enough he could feel her fluttered exhale against his mouth. "It is only pretend."

Perhaps a reminder to himself as much as her.

He skimmed his lips against hers, featherlight. He could feel the ripple of shock go through her—it wasn't what she'd expected. Which left her just enough off-kilter that she met the gentle easing closer with acquiescence.

Mouth still on hers, eyes open as he watched hers flutter closed, he covered one of her fisted hands with his own. He unfurled her fingers as he deepened the kiss, until her lips opened of their own accord, and he could sweep his tongue in to get a taste.

She tasted exotic. Like something rich and foreign and beyond his reach. Which poked at a strange anger deep inside him. Nothing was beyond his reach these days. He did not allow it.

So, he would just have to have her. No anger necessary. No feeling of being thwarted allowed.

He would simply use his excellent patience. Because the groundwork had to be laid first.

So he stepped back, releasing her completely, and then watching everything play out on her face with a fascination he did not quite understand or have a handle on just yet.

Her eyes fluttered open, color high in her cheeks, eyes dark and stormy. Her breathing was uneven as she stood there, still and possibly a little angry. But he wasn't sure if it was him or herself she was angry at.

He could not catalogue anything that made her special or different. He had kissed beauties, innocents and experts alike. He had experienced everything he'd cared to in this life, and yet… She was different and singular, and he could not figure out *why.*

She said nothing, but a wariness crept into her expression to mix with a very clear want. Perhaps he was used to getting what he desired, and she was not. Perhaps that explained this strange dynamic.

"We leave for Mykonos the day after tomorrow," he told her, somewhat brusquely. "I trust you will both be ready."

She did not say anything. He assumed there was some internal fight going on, but she hid it well. Except for the fact she said nothing in response and did not move to go inside. It was the only hint she was fighting off some reaction.

This eased some of the tight, irritating bands around his lungs. Enough he managed a sharp smile.

"Sleep well, *glikí mou*."

And he left her there, adjusting his own plans as he went.

Knowing he would not sleep well at all.

Ari could not deny that nerves assaulted her.

Mother sat on the couch, big sunglasses covering her face, her small bag clutched in her lap. She had agreed to go to the facility, though she'd been a little drunk at the time. But here in the cold light of morning, she had not lodged a complaint. She had done as she was told.

This was not unusual. Mother was not difficult simply to be difficult. When she wasn't drinking, she was… apologetic. Docile. She always promised to do as Ari wanted and to stay away from alcohol and gambling.

In the past, when Ari had been a young child, these promises had sometimes lasted months. But as Ari had gotten older, spent more time at the boxing gym, lived her own life, Mother had backslid.

There was a guilt that lived inside of her because of that, but Ari supposed it matched her mother's guilt for making life difficult.

A pair they were.

"I am not sure I want to go on a plane," Maria said quietly as Ari double-checked her purse even though she knew she had everything. Zervou had said he would be here at nine, which was still fifteen minutes away, but they were both ready.

And clearly nervous.

"Well, I'm afraid you will be getting on one whether you want to or not." Ari said this to her mother as much as she said it to herself. A reminder that, per usual, she had to be the adult in this situation and push them both forward.

"I do not know what this will do, Ari," Mother said softly. "If it is a disease, perhaps it has taken hold so deep there is no cure."

"Perhaps," Ari agreed, because she had learned how to deal with her mother. Arguments did not work. Agreements did not work. Nothing *really* worked, but agreeing with her, placating her at least a little bit, often got them to the next step. "But it is worth a shot."

"At the expense of selling your soul." Maria did not say this bitterly, but Ari felt her bitterness all the same. Not at Ari but at the world.

"I am selling nothing, Mother," Ari replied firmly.

"I would not be so sure." Before Ari could say anything to that, Mother continued, "I know you can protect yourself, though. Keep your guard up."

Ari swallowed down the boiling bitterness. At her mother. At everything. "I always do." What choice did she have?

But the admonition brought back the memory of the way Zervou had kissed her. Was letting him kiss her like that keeping her guard up? Perhaps the kiss itself would have been fine, but she could not seem to stop thinking about it.

No one had ever kissed her like that. Not that she had

much experience. She did not trust men enough to allow such access to her body, but when she'd been younger, softer, there had been times she'd allowed herself to be sweet-talked into a kiss.

Nothing like that. It was like her brain had simply ceased to work. She could think of nothing except the feelings in her body. The heat pumping off of him, the dark, rich taste of him. The way sensation had scattered through her, an explosion of something she did not know how to describe.

Except with one word.

Want.

She was too smart for this, and yet her body and flashes of physical memory did not seem to want to take that on board. She was walking a dangerous line, and usually she avoided dangers that weren't strictly related to a boxing ring, but…

Her mother sat on the couch, purse still clutched in her hands. Nervous, worried, but Ari also saw the hope in her eyes. That somehow, someway, she might be… healed at this facility.

It was worth a million dangerous walks.

So Ari knelt next to her mother. Though this was spurred by vengeance, this opportunity to her mother was just as big, just as important. If she reminded herself of all she stood to gain from this, she could deal with everything else. She *would.*

"I want you to get better," she told her mother earnestly. "This is a chance for that. If we both believe in it."

Maria put her hand on Ari's cheek. Ari's heart throbbed with a terrible ache as her mother's eyes filled. "I am sorry I can't do it on my own," Maria rasped.

Ari shook her head. "No. Do not be sorry." They all knew where the true blame lay. "Be well."

A brisk knock sounded at the door. No doubt Zervou or one of his staff. Ari had to pull herself together, focus on the goal. It had gotten her through. All these years, it had gotten her through.

She got to her feet, not able to meet her mother's worried gaze.

She opened the door to Zervou himself. He was dressed as casually as she'd ever seen him. Still some kind of what she would call dress slacks with a loose button-down fit for Grecian beaches, she supposed.

It made her realize that whatever power he held, that confidence, that assured way he had of moving through life had nothing to do with his clothes or his money and had everything to do with the man he'd built himself into. She envied that. She could manage it in the boxing ring, she thought, but in life, she was always beat right back down again. Could this be the opportunity she'd been looking for, or was it just another step toward being beat down again?

"Are we ready to go?" he asked.

Ari desperately needed to cry, but she could not do it in front of him. So she firmed her jaw, blinked back the tears and met his gaze. "Yes, we are ready."

For whatever came, she would be ready.

CHAPTER SEVEN

THE FLIGHT TO Mykonos was uneventful. Zervou could feel Ariadne's mother glare daggers at him. She'd said nothing to him the entire ride to the airport and now the entire flight, but he didn't need words to understand.

She didn't trust him. No doubt thought he was taking advantage of her daughter. He could almost accept this as fair, even though he was paying to put her into a facility that would allow her daughter not to worry or scrabble for a bit. He was doing them *both* a favor.

It figured, like mother like daughter, that neither fully understood this. Not unlike his own mother.

Except, when they reached the facility, Maria went willingly. Obediently agreeing to every instruction from her daughter and the staff.

Zervou went inside with them, but when it came time to leave Maria in her room, he let Ariadne and her mother have some moments alone to stay goodbye.

It was a nice facility, with some of the best counselors and doctors money could buy. Maria would be in good hands. Perhaps she would even find some sense of healing here that would allow Ariadne to…

Well, he supposed it did not matter. The end result was not his concern. As long as Maria stayed and did not cause trouble during the duration of his plan, and Ariadne could concentrate on their ruse.

That was all he needed to concern himself with.

So he waited outside on a pleasant little patio that overlooked the sea. A quiet, restful place. To his way of thinking, Ariadne could use some quiet and restful. It seemed she had done nothing but struggle her entire life.

Which was neither here nor there except that a rested, settled, happy Ariadne would no doubt draw Erjon out of hiding. Men such as Erjon could not stand for those he considered his property to be happy. Successful. Enjoying *windfalls*. Not without wanting a piece of said windfall.

Especially once he knew who had provided it. The man who'd sent him into hiding in the first place.

Erjon could not, would not hide forever. Zervou held onto this certainty with a certain fanaticism.

The door opened, and Ariadne stepped out into the warmth of a beautiful afternoon. Tears sparkled in her eyes, but she was clearly fighting them back as she approached. "She is settled," she told him firmly, everything she must be feeling carefully controlled behind a stoic mask.

He could not find words for the emotions that seemed to twist and churn in his chest. A kind of yearning, except he did not know how to assuage it. What would make that feeling go away.

So he shoved them away as he rose. "Come, let us go check into our hotel."

She gave a sharp nod, and they walked out to the waiting car. He did not speak on the drive over to the resort, and neither did she. Her mind was no doubt on her mother. His on the strange feelings assaulting him.

It wouldn't do, this strange ignorance of his own emotions. No, if he could not categorize them, they did not belong. He would excoriate them. Somehow.

They arrived at the resort, and his driver took care of everything while Zervou led Ariadne to their private beach villa.

She said nothing, but her eyes were wide as he led her into the spacious private building that would be theirs alone.

"This is not a hotel. This is…" She shook her head. "Something someone as poor as me does not have the vocabulary for."

"Well, consider the next few months a vocabulary lesson."

"Months, is it?"

"As long as it takes. That's what you agreed to, is it not?"

"Yes, as long as it takes." She said it a bit like someone enduring a punishment, which shouldn't frustrate him as much as it did. Her feelings were fairly immaterial to his end goal.

She moved deeper into the room, all the way to the window that dominated the far wall, showing off the pristine white beach and sparkling blue sea. She painted a picture there, mysterious woman staring out at the contrasting beauty of a Greek island. The bright sunlight seemed to make her skin glow, glittering against the hoops in her ears.

There was a potency to her. Something sharp and unique that drew him to move toward her. Yet she continued to be wary of him. Continued to look at him out of the corner of her eye like he might turn into a villain. Which was neither here nor there. Her concerns or feelings didn't matter so much as the end result.

If he reminded himself of this enough, perhaps it would stick.

"You have some time to rest if you'd like. We have reservations for dinner tonight, then tomorrow we will go for a little sail."

She turned to him, nose wrinkled. "Sail?"

"Do you object?" It would make for an excellent photo op, so her objections would be overruled, but that didn't mean he couldn't listen to them.

"I suppose not. I've never been."

He shook his head. "Growing up on the water and never sailing? We will rectify such a shame then."

Her mouth curved ever so slightly. That small smile, as if he'd pleased her, did something very foreign to him. Very…soft.

He found himself frowning. Unsure. But uncertainty was a death knell, and he would not tolerate it.

"How long will we stay?" she asked, eyes back out on the water.

"Two or three days. It depends on if we hear any rumblings of your father. I assume it will take at least an engagement for him to risk being seen, but one never knows for sure."

She nodded along. "And when will this fake engagement occur?"

"When the time is right."

She clearly did not care for that answer. "I have a fight

next month. I can't be…vacationing and eating all the time. I have to prepare. Train."

"This can be arranged around and during vacations. You only need to inform me what you need. All your needs will be met." With a start, he realized he felt that statement a little too deeply, recognizing a feeling he thought he'd eradicated from inside himself.

The need to please, fix, protect…when it was never wanted or reciprocated.

No, he would not fall into that old pattern. He was in charge here. She would take his help, whether she liked it or not. No choices here.

But he could endeavor to make her understand that. "I have no desire to put roadblocks in your life, Ariadne."

She made a considering noise but didn't agree. Which frustrated him, and frustration wouldn't do. So he lightened the mood.

"Consider me more…guardian angel than anything else."

She snorted as he'd expected, rolling her eyes. Giving some humor to the situation so she did not seem quite so…sad.

He did not want her to be sad. He did not want her unsure. Because they would not suit his purposes.

That was all.

After an insanely delicious dinner, they had returned to their private little beach villa, and Ari had retired to her room. She hadn't expected to be able to sleep, still worried about her mother. But something about the large meal and the long day had twined exhaustion with satisfaction, and she drifted off almost the moment her head hit the pillow.

She awoke, groggy and disoriented. But after a few moments of finding her bearings, she realized she felt… rested. Her neck wasn't tight with tension, and she didn't have the usual headache from clenching her jaw in her sleep.

Almost as if good food and a fantastic bed were half of what she was missing in her daily life.

"Well, don't get used to it," she muttered to herself, throwing the covers off.

She had a daily routine, and she had not adhered to it yesterday. So she needed to today. And probably more than just her normal routine considering the amount of food she'd been eating since getting wrapped up in Zervou's orbit.

For a moment, she paused, thinking of him. It all felt like too much—the food, vacation, paying for her own mother to seek treatment for her addictions, but it was just a drop in the bucket for a man with his wealth. And it got her closer to her own personal vendetta. And his.

Something she needed to remind herself of so she did not get caught up thinking he'd been *kind* yesterday. He had simply been a man with money using it to get what he wanted, and since these things were also what she wanted, it was acceptable to go along with it.

In a fight, one did not pull a punch simply because someone else was looking elsewhere. And life was nothing if not a fight. So, she would land whatever punches she needed to with no guilt, no concern.

Take what you need. It's the only way to survive. A motto from her boxing coach when she'd been younger, and she held tight to it now as she surveyed the spacious bedroom.

There was enough room that she could get some preliminary exercises done here. Perhaps there was some kind of fitness center at the main part of the resort, but as she wasn't quite ready to face Zervou this morning to ask, she settled for the floor.

She sat on the rug next to her bed and started with stretches. It felt good to move, to take stock of her body and not feel a boulder of stress in her neck and shoulders. No, it was more like a few pebbles now. They would grow, if she allowed her thoughts to go down that path, but she focused on breathing, stretching, counting instead. Settle into her body. Picture what it could do in a boxing ring.

Once her muscles felt warm, she moved into a plank position, then did pushups, driving herself until her muscles were screaming. She'd need to find some weights at some point today, maybe after *sailing*, but for now she could do the bare minimum with just the weight of her body.

She shifted, moving into a sit-up position. She'd gotten through a handful of these exercises when she saw something move out of the corner of her eye. She glanced over on her way up, only to find Zervou standing in the now open doorway. He wore nothing but a pair of loose-fitting sweatpants low on his hips. His hair was almost tousled.

Everything inside of her seemed to hum to fierce, vibrating life. The definition of his muscles, the trail of dark hair from chest to the waistband of his pants. Her muscles already screaming, but something else fluttering to life to twist and twine with that exertion.

She had been around shirtless men since she'd joined the boxing gym, but this was somehow different. It wasn't work or sport. It was the intimacy of a bedroom. It was a man not prepared to work but simply pulled from sleep.

And maybe, just maybe, it was just *him*. She didn't know what or why, but something about the man Zervou was stoked a strange fire in her she'd never felt. Didn't want to feel.

"There is a facility downstairs for such things," he said, his voice low and sleep rasped. "You need not thump away."

For a moment, she could not seem to find her voice. Her tongue felt…heavy and twisted up. Heat that had nothing to do with the exercises she'd been doing settled in her cheeks. "I woke you up." Which was an utterly ridiculous thing to say.

"Yes. You did."

Ari managed to clear her throat, find some semblance of herself instead of this strange woman who could not find her footing with him. "I cannot eat as we have been eating and not exercise. I have to maintain my weight. And my strength."

"Use the gym then, Ariadne." He turned and walked away, the play of muscles on his back as he moved their own mesmerizing dance.

She let out a careful breath, frustrated with herself for the shake in it.

Okay, so he was attractive. She'd known that before she'd seen him without his shirt. Having the actual picture of what those muscles looked like when not encased in fabric changed absolutely nothing.

Except some elemental thing inside of her. Somehow.

She shook that ridiculous thought away and abandoned her sit-ups. A run would be better. She thought clearer after a run.

So she followed him out of the room and into the grand dining area where windows showed off breathtaking views of a pastel sunrise. Added to that was a beautiful breakfast spread already filling the table. Which seemed impossible since she hadn't seen or heard a hint of anyone else here besides them.

She supposed he paid handsomely for that kind of invisible service. What a life.

He plucked a piece of fruit from one plate and popped it into his mouth as he walked past, making no effort to dress or cover himself. He went over to a coffeepot, grabbed himself a mug and poured.

"I need to go for a run," she informed him, not sure what she felt. Uncomfortable, yes, but it was more complicated than that. Like this was some strange intimacy they had certainly not earned.

He didn't say anything at first, took a sip of the coffee instead. Then he pointed to a chair. "First, you will eat. I will have some coffee like a civilized human being. And then we will go for a run together."

She eyed him critically. Endurance was part of boxing, and she could run for hours if she had the right preparation. "It's clear you keep yourself fit, but I am an athlete. I'm not sure you'll be able to keep up."

Something in that sleepy gaze sharpened, a change that arrowed inside of her like a tuning fork. "A challenge? I accept."

"I wasn't..."

"Sit. Eat. One shouldn't run on an empty stomach. An *athlete* should know such things."

Yes, an athlete should. And she often did her level best to fuel her body, but there wasn't always money, time or inclination.

But right now, in this moment, there was a huge breakfast spread, and her stomach was rumbling, even though it shouldn't considering how much she'd eaten last night.

Still, she sat and picked out the healthier items. A bowl of fruit, some yogurt with a healthy mix of nuts and honey. She forced herself to pass on the pastries no matter how delicious they looked. She could hardly go into her next match above weight. She considered coffee but opted for water.

"No coffee?"

"I am not much of a coffee drinker."

He made a sound of disapproval, filling his plate as he did. Then sitting down next to her despite the fact it was a large table, and he could have sat anywhere.

She pretended like she didn't notice. "Where will we run?" she asked between bites of yogurt.

"The beach is as good a place as any. A better workout, no?"

"I suppose."

"How long would you like to go?"

"A few miles should be sufficient. You needn't—"

"I usually do five if I have the inclination and the beach at hand."

Five. She studied him more carefully. Without his shirt, it was obvious he must spend some time keeping himself in shape. It couldn't just be running—though she imagined heavy cardio helped define the muscle tone, but there had to be some weightlifting. Something to make those shoulders as impressive as they were.

"Is five too many?" he asked, a note to his voice akin to teasing, and when she managed to tear her gaze from his arm, she understood why.

He knew she was ogling him. She refused to be embarrassed or tried to refuse anyway, but she felt a telltale heat in her cheeks. The embarrassment she tried to ignore intensified.

She never blushed. "Five sounds good for a start," she muttered into her yogurt. "I will need to change." She rose, leaving part of her breakfast untouched. She needed to start making sacrifices to maintain weight. Maybe after her bout next month she could go a little lax for a bit, but for now, she had to focus on who she would be for the fight.

Back in her room, she rummaged through her suitcase that wasn't really hers, because Zervou had purchased it and filled it with the wardrobe he thought she might need. Luckily, she had brought her own athletic wear. She changed into shorts and a sports bra. At home, she would have pulled a T-shirt on over it, but this was the beach. It would be hot.

And you want to show off.

With that uncomfortable thought, she grabbed a light T-shirt and threw it on before lacing up her running shoes and heading back out to the main room to meet Zervou.

He was ready, if the laced-up running shoes were anything to go by, but he still wore no shirt. *He is most assuredly showing off.* She couldn't help but remember that night she'd gone to his house in Corfu and his parting shot.

The deal is not about sex. But it is hardly off the table if you should decide you're interested.

She could not afford to be interested. It would be a risk with absolutely no reward except a few seconds of pleasure—hardly reward enough when something like chocolate cake and the heady adrenaline of a win in the boxing ring existed.

So she would not allow herself to be distracted. This was training. If he wanted to flaunt his flawless body, that was his business and had absolutely nothing to do with her.

He led her out a back door onto a patio, then downstairs onto a beach. Farther down, she could see people with their bright umbrellas and towels crowding the sandy area, but down here there was no one but them. Since private beaches weren't legal by any stretch of the imagination, she could only roll her eyes at the whims of the wealthy.

"I have a route all planned out. You only need to follow me."

So she did. And he was right. The sand offered a more strenuous workout, which she was grateful for, but having a running companion meant her usual thinking time was shot. Because instead of thinking of anything she should, she was watching the way he ran.

He might not be a professional athlete, but there was a natural athleticism to his stride. A determined intensity to his run. To his everything. It echoed in her, these strange waves of heat and want and things she had not allowed herself to ever explore.

Men were dangerous to women. Sex was dangerous for women. She had been on guard her whole life.

But what if this was a respite to all that *on guard*?

The idea of it, the possibility of it, caused a yearning inside her—one that she was all too familiar with. Because Ari's life was a study in the things she wanted and couldn't have.

Or had been.

Because Zervou was offering something else, wasn't he? She was in Mykonos. She had dined well the past week. She had new clothes, and her mother was in a beautiful facility trying to heal.

It was a windfall of things she wanted, so why not… keep wanting and getting?

The deal is not about sex. But it is hardly off the table if you should decide you're interested.

If she was considering this a rest from many of her obligations, knowing it would all be taken away once Zervou got what he wanted—which, luckily enough was what she wanted—why not enjoy it all? The vacations? The clothes? The money? The time not worrying about her mother or her debts?

And maybe, just maybe, these physical reactions in her body.

Maybe.

CHAPTER EIGHT

THEY RETURNED TO Corfu after a few beautiful days in Mykonos. Zervou dropped Ariadne off at her little hovel of an apartment and, since she was busy during the day with her training and teaching, planned a week of dinners.

Then found himself somewhat restless when he dropped her off every night in this unsafe neighborhood. He had his security team develop a detail to ensure she was safe—in the apartment, on her way to and from the gym or the store or whatever else she busied herself with.

He did not inform her of this. It was just…good sense on his part, so required neither permission nor approval. Who knew how Erjon would reappear? He might come to make threats to his daughter first, and that would not do for Zervou's plans.

So her safety, her poor living conditions should not take over his thoughts, but he found himself thinking about it far too often. The danger she put herself in, no matter how capable she might be of taking care of herself, defending herself. It all seemed so much more work than necessary.

Which was none of his concern. All that mattered to him was her safety so he could lure her father out and crush him. The goal was Erjon and Erjon alone, of whom there had still been no sighting. No hint of him.

So each week the relationship with Ariadne would have to escalate—in the press, in how they were seen. He would have to find new ways to reach whatever corners of Greece or Europe or *wherever* Erjon hid himself.

Pictures of them sailing had made their way to a few online gossip sites. Just him piloting the small boat and her lounging in the sun. A big hat had covered her face, but every site named her and mentioned she was a well-known boxer in Corfu.

Ariadne had studied the photos last night on his phone while they'd dined at a high-profile restaurant. The makeup she'd worn had not quite covered the black eye she'd been sporting, but he did not bring it up.

She received such injuries in the course of her training, and even though he found his gaze attracted to this physical mark time and time again, he could hardly find fault with it. She was in a physical profession. She would suffer bodily injury—in practice, in her bouts.

He did not understand how that knowledge seemed to stay in his gut like a hard, painful rock when it was simply a fact of her life. One that mattered to him *not at all.*

He tried to busy himself during the days with work on the new stadium, plans for the sporting events it would house once complete. But such things only led him to think of boxing and Ariadne. This was the center of her world—particularly now that her mother was tucked away in a facility.

For a brief moment, Zervou found himself wondering what it would be like to have a passion, a center of his world that was not simply domination and destruction of his enemies.

Then he laughed at himself. What a pointless existence.

But as the week wore on, nothing changed. He spent too much of his day thinking about her, wondering how she filled her days. Boxing, mostly, he knew from having his security team keep an eye on her.

He wanted to watch her box again. The glimpse he'd gotten of her initially had been intriguing.

And what was stopping him, he asked himself one sunny afternoon.

Absolutely nothing.

He called for Bacchus and had his car pulled around. He didn't take any of his men this time. Maybe he didn't want to spend time in desperate neighborhoods that reminded him of being a child, but the boxing gym was different. The desperation wasn't so thick there.

People were too busy fighting.

When he arrived, he couldn't have been more pleased with his timing. Much like the first time he'd tracked her down, Ariadne was in the ring, wearing the necessary gear. Her hair hidden under the padding, no doubt in those tight braids. It looked to be early in the practice round as she hadn't even worked up a sweat yet, but she moved on her feet, light and graceful.

He didn't think she'd noticed his arrival yet, so he stayed where he was near the entrance to the room.

He had not touched her again since that kiss outside her apartment after their first official outing. The photographs of sailing and dining the other night had certainly given an air of intimacy, but they had not been overt.

It hadn't been necessary for his purposes just yet, though that was a good next step. Some kind of picture of, at the very least, an embrace. Something to make its way to Erjon. Something to get the man planning to make his return. He would, Zervou knew he would.

But Zervou wasn't thinking about Ariadne's father as he watched her bounce, duck, jab. She made good contact with her sparring partner's chin. A woman this time, who stumbled back but immediately hopped from foot to foot as she raised her gloves back to her face.

They weren't going full force, even his untrained eye could see that. Perhaps they were practicing footwork more than punches and feints. Perhaps they were practicing it all. If he could drag his gaze away from Ariadne to study the other woman as well, maybe he'd be able to figure it out.

Instead he watched the ripple of muscle along Ariadne's arms. The strength in her legs as she dodged a blow and then the simple, brutal grace of returning her own. It glanced off the other woman's chin—clearly pulled as the woman barely reacted.

A buzzer sounded, and when they both stepped away from each other and began to remove their gloves and headgear, he realized it had been some kind of timer.

The women dropped their equipment, then stood in the middle of the ring talking. The other woman's expression was animated, her gestures wide as she spoke to Ariadne. Zervou found himself fascinated by the expression on Ariadne's face.

Nothing guarded. None of that wariness he was so used to seeing. Everything in her expression was bright and engaged. She nodded along, offered replies Zervou couldn't hear. Then the woman said something, and Ariadne… laughed.

It was as if all other sound ceased to exist as the echo of her uninhibited, husky laugh made its way to him. Nothing bitter in it. Nothing scathing. Just a pure, happy laugh.

It was the strangest moment, because the sound seemed to land with all the force of a blow, penetrating his chest almost painfully. The only thing he could think to liken it to was the force of the bullet he'd watched slam into his father's chest.

But it was not a searing pain, or overwhelming fear that ripped through him in this moment. No. It was a dark, clawing need to possess. It was as potent as the need to avenge his father—a goal all these years in the making.

And with both, she was the key.

When she happened to glance over, eyes meeting his, for a moment, it felt like she was the key to everything.

But the ease went out of her expression, and a hint of tension crept into her shoulders.

Frustration filtered into the strange weightless place he'd been. Why should she tense at his arrival? Why should she still look at him with distrust? It was insulting. Infuriating.

And still the pounding need of *want* echoed inside of him like a drum. An eternal beat that had always existed, would always exist. Had existed before her, just waiting to be brought to life.

She turned her attention back to her sparring partner. They spoke for a few more minutes, then collected their gear and got out of the ring. While the other woman headed for the locker room—after tossing a curious glance at him over her shoulder—Ariadne came his way.

"What's up?" she asked on approach, studying him as though she did not trust any reason he would be here. Her braids were tight, but a few hairs escaped to corkscrew around her face. She was sweaty, a little out of breath, and the claws of need only dug deeper.

"We are going dancing tonight." Because he wanted his hands on her, and if it was in the name of being seen, he'd decided that was excuse enough.

"Are we?" she returned, eyeing him with that patent wariness that threatened to set his teeth on edge.

"Yes. When you are finished, I will drive you to my estate. I have everything you need to get ready."

He braced himself for the argument, the refusal. More of that damn pride to get in his way. He prepared to refuse any and all of her potential rejections. This was what must be done, and she had agreed to his plan, so she did not get to say no.

But she offered no rejections or refusals. After a long study of him, she simply shrugged. "All right. I'll be out in a few."

Ari stood in one of the bathrooms in Zervou's house—if one could call this room the size of her apartment something as simple as a bathroom, or this entire place something as simple as a *house*—studying herself in the mirror.

She wasn't quite sure how she felt about what she saw. On the one hand, she had been taught since she'd been a child not to dress to entice the wrong kind of attention—something she'd begun to realize in her teens was just a false sense of security. Men would be awful no matter what a woman wore.

But it was still a hard mental habit to break. She tended to dress to exaggerate her muscles and downplay the more feminine aspects to her body. She was used to that, comfortable with that, so the brevity of her dress was…awkward almost.

On the other hand, she liked the way she looked in her reflection. She loved boxing and the way it made her feel—strong, powerful, capable of taking any blow. But sometimes, on the rare moments she could think of something beyond survival, the side effects of boxing left her feeling…ugly. Undesirable. Her crooked nose, the bruises, the swelling.

It was why she'd gotten the nose ring and then the belly ring. The pieces of jewelry made her feel…something. She didn't have all the words for it. Just more herself—a dichotomy of things. Not just muscle and bone, waiting to be crashed into.

There was more to her than survival. Than fight.

This dress added to a sense that she was *more*, because she looked…sexy. There really wasn't much to the outfit. The skirt was brief, the neckline low. It emphasized her muscular frame, but with the right hairdo and makeup, she could soften that. Make it alluring instead of intimidating. Or perhaps both.

Either way, it was an outfit—particularly with the heels—that would draw attention. She was so used to avoiding attention, it felt a mix of rebellious—a good, exhilarating feeling—and *wrong*—an uncomfortable amount of nervousness she didn't like at all.

She could take care of herself, so drawing attention

wasn't such a risk, she reminded herself. Especially since Zervou would be there. She could take all sorts of risks with him as her companion for the evening.

Which led to an uncomfortable realization.

She'd begun to trust him. A mistake, surely, but it was just sort of there. A natural conclusion to enjoying spending dinners with him.

He was slick and arrogant but had a cutting kind of humor to him. She hadn't seen him enjoy hurting anyone or go out of his way to try to wield his wealth or power. He knew what he wanted and made it happen—and she couldn't help but respect that. She'd do more of it if she could.

And then there was the way he looked at her. The way he would look at her in this dress. Much the same way he looked at her while she was boxing.

She knew what professional interest looked like—what that male gaze was searching for when a man studied her as a boxer. She also recognized the look of a fragile male ego who wanted to conquer. She knew how all sorts of ways people looked at her when she boxed.

Nothing like Zervou. Nothing with any kind of sexual pull. Maybe she didn't know a thing about sex, but she knew that this feeling could only have to do with that.

Which meant she was walking a dangerous line. But that was nothing new, she reminded herself before stepping out of the bathroom into the spacious, bright guest bedroom that looked out over Corfu.

She had never even thought to picture herself up here, in a fancy house. She hadn't even considered being lucky enough to *work* at a place such as this. Never once in her life. Her dreams were much more realistic and humble.

Fight to survive. The extent of her dreams had been rest. And, okay, revenge on the father who'd caused so much of her struggle.

Now she was in this mansion as a kind of…guest.

Zervou stood looking out the window, hands behind his back. Tall. Still. Outrageously handsome and sure of everything he did. Powerful.

How she ached to have some kind of power over her life. Perhaps that was what made being in his orbit more and more enjoyable. Perhaps that was what made him feel something close to irresistible.

"We might need to discuss how appropriate some of your clothing choices are," she said to his back.

He turned slowly. He said nothing at first. His dark, fierce eyes did the talking. His gaze took a tour. And took its time.

She liked that. There was no denying the heat in his eyes sparked some heat inside her. Some primitive desire. Knowing he found her some kind of enticing made her *feel* enticing.

His gaze made her wonder what it would be like for his hands to take the same path. Would she let him tonight? Would he offer? He had barely touched her since that kiss. Oh, he'd done plenty of looking, but his hands and body had remained resolutely to himself.

It had to be a purposeful choice, though she didn't know why.

When his eyes met hers, and it felt like some kind of mini explosion erupting between them, she figured she didn't need to know why he waited. Even if not tonight, some kind of offer seemed inevitable.

Necessary.

"I cannot identify one problem with what you're wearing. I have excellent taste."

She laughed in spite of herself. *So* arrogant.

His smile in return was sharp. Predatory.

Why did pleasure receptors across her abdomen seem to spring to life at that?

"It is a club. The attire is meant to be…" Again his gaze took a tour of her body. She felt…electrified, but pleasantly. A buzzing. A throbbing deep in her body. "Breathable. For dancing."

Breathable. She rolled her eyes. What rot. But she didn't argue with him. She instead followed him through his ridiculous house and out to the ridiculous garage full of vehicles. "Do you have this many cars at…where do you live full-time?"

"Wherever I like," he returned.

"But surely you have a home base," she said, sliding into the car after he'd opened the door for her.

He came around and got in the driver seat. He hadn't driven them to any of their dinners. It was a strange change of pace. It made everything feel more…intimate. Real.

Now that *is going too far.*

"Home base? No." He shook his head as if the idea was ludicrous. "I follow the business. Buy property wherever feels optimal. Or enjoyable. There is no need for a base when you are rich."

Optimal. The word was so devoid of any emotion. Not that she had any great love for her home base, but it was home. It was…the ground from which she'd grown. Her roots were tangled in the poor, desperate soil.

"Where did you grow up then?" she asked him, wanting some sense of who he was at those roots. Maybe then she'd have a better handle on him.

"A small village near the Bulgarian border," he replied somewhat flatly.

"Do you ever go back?"

There was a pause. She might have called it a hesitation except it was nearly impossible to believe Zervou hesitated over anything. "My mother and grandmother live there still," he said.

Which didn't exactly answer her question, did it? She opened her mouth to ask another probing question, but he spoke before she could.

"How is your mother faring?" he asked as he navigated the Friday evening traffic in Corfu. A clear attempt to change the subject. Away from him. Onto her.

She didn't think he cared in any deep sense, but it still meant something to her that he would ask—even as a distraction. It meant he understood enough to know it mattered to her. Perhaps it was all a great ruse, but he was a good actor in it.

Enjoy, remember? Maybe even enjoy the acting. As long as you understand it's temporary. And wasn't she an expert at understanding temporary? Her life was built on the shifting sands of other people's whims, vices or fists. So she did not need to know him or probe under the ruse or the change of subjects. He could be a mystery to her. It changed nothing.

"She is…well, I think. It is a difficult process, even in the lap of luxury. She has no complaints about the facility."

"Then what does she have complaints about?"

She studied his profile, surprised he could read what she wasn't saying. Surprised he would call her out on it.

In the end, she shrugged. What did it matter if he knew her mother's concerns? "The more sober she is, the more aware she is and the less she likes the idea of you paying her way. Or what she imagines I am doing to pay for you paying her way."

"You did not tell her about our arrangement?"

"Regarding Erjon? No. I never mention him to her." She stared out at the passing city. "And I never will, even if we are successful. She will think we had a grand love affair and it ended."

"*When* we are successful, *glikí mou*. I will not be giving up until Erjon is begging for mercy and perhaps not even then."

He said that with a dark fervor she appreciated. She also would not give up. Not until Erjon paid. Not until he suffered. It was a good talisman amid this strange turn her life had taken. As long as her mother was safe and Ari had boxing and the chance to ruin her father, all was well.

Zervou drove them to the back of the club. At what must have been some kind of private entrance, they were greeted by a man Ari thought might be the owner. A manager at the very least. He led them inside where the music pumped, the beat reverberating through not just the club but her entire body.

She'd never had time for clubs. For frivolous. She was fascinated. But she was also surprised because this was not exactly the place for a photo op, with the low lighting and the crush of bodies. She supposed not everything had to be about a picture. Still, she was curious what had prompted this choice, much different than the ones he'd made so far.

It was clear the club owners knew Zervou and were eager to please. They were shown to a private corner. Though it took Ari a few moments of sitting there to realize it, someone had been installed just a few steps from their booth to act as a kind of security so no one approached them unbidden.

When the waitress arrived, Zervou ordered some drink Ari had never even heard of, but she had no doubt it was alcoholic, so she stopped the waitress before she hopped off eager to do a rich man's bidding.

"I would like a club soda."

"Oh. Of course." The waitress smiled politely then bounced off.

"What I ordered was meant to be shared, Ariadne," Zervou said with some disapproval.

"I will not drink alcohol," she said firmly. There was no reason to partake in that which had taken so much from her mother. She braced for an argument. A lecture at the very least.

"Very well," he said instead. "Will you dance?"

She looked out at the gyrating bodies. The thud of music. She glanced at him, felt that sizzle of his gaze on hers.

Yes, she would very much like to dance with him, to feel his body against hers in a kind of safe environment. A test, perhaps.

Still, she had never really danced before.

"I will, but I have never really danced. I cannot promise it will be much of a photo op, if that is why we're here." Maybe it was a *little* fishing, but he didn't bite.

“Dancing is not so complicated. Especially here. Think of it as a boxing match,” he offered. He pointed out to the crowd. “See the woman in bright pink?”

Ari spotted her, a pretty blonde in a dress that stood out even in the dimmer light. She was being led out to the dance floor by a short man with his hair slicked back.

“It begins with a bob and a weave,” Zervou said, with some humor. “He pulls her in, she returns with a duck, a break.”

Amused at the boxing terms being used to describe the couple’s dancing, Ari kept watching as Zervou narrated.

“He feints, then moves in, but she parries. Gives him a paw—nothing real. No, she likes the dance, but she’s not going for the knockout.”

“I guess it depends on what you consider the knockout in dancing. She’s got her clinch,” Ari said. “Maybe that was the KO all along.” She turned her attention from the couple to him, found herself grinning. Which was just…strange.

There was a strange weightlessness to these days. Even with training, she didn’t have to worry about her mother. Whether the facility did its job or not, Mom was safe and couldn’t get into bigger trouble or drag Ari into trouble she couldn’t talk or pay her way out of. Ari didn’t have to worry about money or groceries—both because Zervou kept feeding and clothing her and because her mother wasn’t here to gamble it away. For the first time in her entire life, she didn’t have to worry about anything except her training.

And perhaps the physical reaction she had to the man who was supposed to help her end her father.

"Come," he instructed, standing and holding out his hand for her to take.

So she did. Let him guide her out to the crush of bodies. Like the woman in pink, she did a bob, a weave, a feint, making him laugh—a low sound that rumbled through her like fire.

But then he pulled her into the hard heat of his body, in time with the pulsing beat around them. The dress he'd chosen for her offered a cutout of skin at her back and abdomen, and his hand found the spot on her back.

If drinking alcohol felt as good as his hands on her skin, maybe she could understand her mother's addiction. Maybe she could understand a lot of things that had previously been out of her reach.

Chalk it up to life experiences. As dangerous and ephemeral as boxing. She was well-versed in all the sacrifices a person had to make for the high of victory. She found it worth it. Every single time.

He pointed to their table, so she turned to look. "Our drinks have come," he said into her ear.

They could go back, sip their drinks, talk, but she liked this. The way it felt like boxing and life and a million other things she'd never been able to allow herself.

He was behind her as she swayed to the music, ignoring the drinks, and she did the most out-of-character thing she could think of.

She allowed herself to lean back into him, the strong, muscular wall of him. She reached back, hooked an arm around his neck and swayed to the erotic beat of the music. He had one hand on her hip, while one arm came around her, just under her breasts, with a large possessive hand pressed right where the little cutout of her dress bared her skin.

"Let's keep dancing," she said. Her stomach shivered under the weight of his hand. A pulsing need throbbed through her entire body. They swayed, and she could feel the heat of him seep into her. She could feel the hard length of him against the small of her back. An erotic thrill.

He was Zervou Kritikos, and *she* had this effect on him. So she leaned into it, even more into him, into the sway of bodies. She let her body move with his, against his. Reveled in the sensations spreading out across the expanse of her bare skin.

When one song moved into the other, she made no move to return to their table or the drinks. She kept her arm hooked around him, his front to her back. Their bodies fitted together, her heart beating in time with the music and his breath against her ear.

"Are you teasing me, *glikí mou*?" His voice was a rumbled caress against her ear.

"Sounds like a dangerous proposition," she replied. "A risk, to tease someone such as you."

"Indeed. I would suggest being ready to accept the consequences of such behavior." His hand moved down her abdomen, her muscles contracting at the contact. Gentle fingers traced the hoop at her belly button, but there was nothing gentle about the grip his other hand had on her hip.

She liked the contrast. The heat. The adrenaline pumping through her veins and echoing in her ears along with the beat of the music. She liked watching the sea of people drink, laugh, dance while she could only feel Zervou behind her, feel him touch her, his breath against her ear.

She knew there were two roads here. Enjoy this moment, go back to their table and accept it was all pretend. She could also take a slight detour.

The deal is not about sex. But it is hardly off the table if you should decide you're interested.

Not a deviation, not a change of direction, just a nice little…side quest.

"Perhaps I will like the consequences," she decided aloud.

That grip on her hip tightened, sending another bolt of thrill and want through her. "Then I suggest we go somewhere more private."

She glanced over her shoulder at him, met that smoldering gaze. "Lead the way."

CHAPTER NINE

ZERVOU WAS HARD and aching and maintained control only because he was determined not to be some sex-crazed teenager. He was made of sterner stuff, no matter how alluring, desirable, enticing and unexpected his little boxing siren was.

He considered finding a private room here in the club, but that would be quick. Enjoyable but quick.

No, he'd rather like to spend his time on Ariadne Malis. Explore that fascinating athlete's body of hers in the light. In his bed. She would not change her mind. It wasn't in her nature. She had decided she wanted to explore the heat between them, so he could take his time.

Drinks forgotten, he led her right back out the way they'd come. He'd leave a hefty tip for the waitress. Later.

He didn't wait for the valet, found the car himself and eased it out of the parking garage.

"We weren't there for very long," she said. She sounded so much like herself, not winded or breathy or moved by the moment while they were dancing. But her eyes were a little wild.

He focused on her eyes. Then the road as he sped through Corfu and back to his estate. Yes, he would have her there. All night. "Long enough to be seen. That's what is necessary."

"And what is this?" she asked.

"It feels rather necessary, does it not?"

She let out a slow breath. "It does," she agreed.

And then said nothing else as they drove back the way they'd come, with perhaps a little shred of recklessness.

When he pulled the car into the garage, nothing had changed in the raging swirl of sensations inside of him. She got out without waiting for him to come around and open the door for her. So they met in the middle.

There was a moment, yet another moment he could not articulate to himself, of standing here in the dim light of a garage staring at her. Her staring back.

He wanted his hands on her, and yet here they stood. Separated by space and something else he couldn't identify. Like they were standing on opposite sides of a line that they had to choose to cross. A line that couldn't be uncrossed. That could change everything.

But how utterly ridiculous. He was Zervou Kritikos. He had built himself up into a billionaire. Impenetrable. Unstoppable. He crossed whatever lines he chose and uncrossed them just as decisively.

So he moved to her and felt vindicated when the usual wariness she regarded him with did not appear. Because this was something besides their…business deal, their pretend for the world, for Erjon.

This was just them.

So he took her hand once more and led her through the garage, into the peaceful estate that had begun to grow on him.

This wasn't wrong or a distraction, because this had been simmering from the very beginning. Always an option. Always a nice little detour possibility. It changed nothing.

He wouldn't let it, no matter how seismic everything felt inside of him.

Once inside, he pushed her up against the wall. He was bigger than her, no doubt stronger simply because of the size of him. But she knew how to fight. She knew how to land a punch.

But she acquiesced to him. Her mouth, her body. Accepting him, softening around him.

It was a thrill to possess her, to control her. This woman who delivered and accepted punches for a living, writhed against him as though he had all the answers. As though her pride did not matter because she would allow him to take care of everything.

Everything.

"I chose this dress specifically," he told her, surprised at the unfamiliar edge to his own voice.

She blinked up at him, lips swollen from his kiss, eyes foggy with desire and something else he couldn't quite put his finger on, but he put that aside for the moment. He lowered to his knees in front of her.

"Did you know I cannot stop thinking about this? Just a tiny little hoop. And it haunts me." He pressed a kiss at the bared midsection, just below her navel.

She made a noise in the back of her throat. Pleasure and need. And while his mouth played with the soft skin around her belly button, the impressive muscle beneath, his hand slid up her inner thigh, until he felt her tremble.

For a moment, she stiffened, clenched her legs together before relaxing.

It was the first little alarm bell, easily flicked away when he reached the heated apex of her thighs. So sweet. So ready.

"I can feel how much you want me. Tell me."

"I..." She couldn't seem to get the words out, but she moved against his hand, held onto him. Gave *over* to him as his fingers found his way around the fabric covering her and into the molten heat of her.

It was a power unlike any he had ever experienced. The sounds she made, how easy it was to stir, tease, then send her quick and sharp over that glorious edge.

He looked up at her. She was dazed. Disoriented. Like she didn't quite know what she'd gotten herself into. Like no one had ever touched her quite like that.

He could have her, right here. Its own bout of rough and quick and shocking. But he'd left the club for something in particular. Quick and needy had its place, but not this first time.

Perhaps only time. Perhaps it was all they'd be given, all they'd need.

He doubted it, and still...

"No, not here," he muttered, more to himself than her. He took her by the hand and led her deeper into the house. It would be in a bed. He would take his damn time.

In the bedroom, he kissed her again. Hungry gulps of that taste he'd never before found anywhere. She kissed him back, but as his hand roamed, explored, hers...didn't return the favor. She didn't seem to know what to do with them, even as she pressed her body to his, kissed him back with the same intensity, but something was just not…quite right.

He'd expected graceful, like she was in the boxing ring. Maybe combative, but certainly at ease. And yet there was some…odd tension in her.

He pulled his mouth away, stared down at her.

Her cheeks flushed, her pulse scrabbling as she breathed heavily. She appeared every inch the interested and willing participant, but something was…off. Unpracticed. An uncertainty she showed in almost nothing else. Except that which she'd never done before—balance on a boat, eat lobster and…this.

"Surely not," he muttered, as the idea took root in his mind.

She looked away. "Why are you stopping?" she demanded. But she did not meet his gaze anymore.

His body raged, ached. A part of him wanted, with no concern for what he might be taking. But there was a larger part of him too aware of the power imbalances in the world. He would take care of everything for her, but did she trust that, believe that?

"I do not despoil virgins." It came out harsher than he intended, but it seemed the only way to find his control. His sense.

She rolled her eyes, managed to glare at him, but the color in her cheeks spoke of more than passion now. "Despoil? Get a grip. I hardly consider myself *spoiled* should I let you put yourself inside me."

It was a bit crude but not wrong he supposed. And confirmation of what he was concerned about. Concerned, though not…altogether against. "Then why have you not…?"

"Are you so sheltered you cannot say the words, Zervou?" she asked, mocking him. "Why have I not *had sex* before?"

He was shocked into having absolutely no retort for that. Not the words, but the distasteful mocking in her tone.

"Because the world is a dangerous place," she told him, with a flatness that definitely spoke of experience in danger. "And I have only had myself to protect me from this world. I suppose it might be smarter to protect myself from you, but I was rather looking forward to… not having to for once."

Because she would let him protect her, this fierce creature. That was what she meant. She trusted him enough to allow him to protect her. That thing he'd always desired.

It made his decision for him. And it was a decision, a choice. He was in control. And he would protect.

"You said you I could use you. And you would use me." She made a gesture to the space between them. "Is that not what this is?"

Use. It was not the right word at all, but he hardly knew what the right word would be. So he ignored it. "Be sure this is what you want," he told her, commanded her.

She met his gaze. Direct and fierce. "I am always sure."

It was only the tiniest bit of a lie. Ari was mostly sure. Almost totally. She wasn't certain there wouldn't be a regret or two on the other side of this, but she could live with regrets.

She herself was the embodiment of her mother's regrets, was she not? Regret was simply an act of living. Like breathing. There were no choices, really.

Depressing thought. She wanted to go back to what she'd felt at the club. Somehow both powerful and entirely taken care of. That she was in charge, but he was handling everything, and she was free to simply enjoy.

The fact he'd seen the virgin on her was embarrassing. Not that avoiding engaging in sex was embarrassing—she knew her reasons. They had been good reasons and choices. The embarrassment was…something else.

Not shame. Perhaps just the discomfort in it being obvious she didn't know how to do something when she had to know how to do everything.

And she didn't like that at all. But if they could go back to the way he'd touched her in the crush of bodies, if she could feel that hard line of his body atop hers… the embarrassment would fade. The pleasure would return. And she could chase all these physical sensations to what people claimed was *quite* the end result.

So she moved into him again, wrapping her arms around his neck and throwing everything she had into the kiss.

It erupted, exploded, ebbed and flowed again and again, his hands streaking over her. She didn't quite know what to do with her own, but she had a flash of him running on that beach in Mykonos. Of the way his muscles moved. She wanted to touch. To see.

So she began to unbutton his shirt as his mouth devoured hers. The heat and reaction to his hands in her most intimate places in his *entry way* overwhelmed every rational thought.

She hadn't even made it down the row of buttons when he wrenched his mouth from hers, then turned her, hands sure and certain and in control.

She liked that, too. She was so used to being on edge, waiting for someone to land a blow, but she didn't have to worry here. He had her.

He undid the tie on the back of the dress, smoothed it off of her as his hands followed the trail of fabric all the way down. There'd been no way to wear a bra under the dress, so she was in nothing but her underwear, and he was still fully dressed, only his shirt unbuttoned.

Not that she could see him. He stood behind her, his hands on her shoulders.

"You have bruises," he said, and she could not quite read his tone. Almost accusatory, but she did not think he was accusing *her*.

"Pretty much always. Comes with the job." For the first time in ages, perhaps ever, she wondered what it would be like to walk through the world without some kind of ache or pain or mark from what she'd chosen to do.

He made a sound, somewhat frustrated, then brushed a featherlight touch against the one on the side of her rib cage.

She shivered, leaning back into him once again. He held her upright, gentle pressure on her hips. Then he brushed his mouth across one of the bruises on her side, just above her waist, and her breath caught. So gentle. So strange. So wonderful. She couldn't see what he was doing, and it heightened the touch, the anticipation.

A featherlight touch across her lower back, along the

row of hoops in her ears, then his lips along the side of her neck, then teeth.

"Zervou." She didn't know what else to say. She didn't have the vocabulary for this, for her wants, her needs.

But he did. Surely he did.

"Lie down."

The order sent a delicious thrill through her, but she was also not very used to taking orders. "Aren't you supposed to be naked, too?"

"Lie down, Ariadne."

There was a warning note to his voice that echoed inside her like a throb. So she did as she was told. She crawled onto the bed and lay down.

He stood on the side of the bed, surveying her. His eyes hot and fierce and as weighty as any touch. But he didn't touch her, and she didn't reach out to touch him. Something about the anticipation made the ache dig deeper, want more. Something about waiting for him to set the tone seemed like it would make everything that much more…explosive.

After excruciating, wonderful moments of his eyes touring her body, he shrugged out of his shirt. Then undid his pants and pushed them off. He said nothing, but his eyes never left her as he took all of his clothes off.

Unreasonably handsome. Sharp as any blade. Strong and broad and so…*big*. She had no experience with size, but this felt…impossible.

Wonderful.

He sheathed himself in a condom, never taking his eyes off of her. She felt that gaze like a weight. For a brief moment, the sheer size of him made her wonder if she knew what the hell she was doing.

And then he was ranging over her, that dark, fierce gaze as potent as any alcohol, she was quite sure. Because she forgot her concerns. She forgot everything except the vibrating want in her body.

He'd made her fall apart with just his hand, and that had been a revelation. What might this be?

He did not ask her if she was sure again. Perhaps he could see it in her. Perhaps he did not care. He was just suddenly *there*, nudging his way in.

Ari knew all about pain, about letting her body relax and accept. And in doing so, the intimate stretch, the sensuous, slow move from two to one, did not so much hurt as settle. From the knee-jerk *I can't* to *yes. This. Always.*

And he moved into her, with her. So that they were a wave together, crashing slowly, passionately into shore, into pleasure and dazzling, exquisite falls. Up and over again, and again, and again.

He said her name, a low growl in her ear. She was shuddering, overwhelmed by sensation, by something akin to joy. He pushed deep inside her one last time, shuddering himself.

She had brought a man like Zervou to shudders, and *that* was power.

She closed her eyes. She had put her body to the test time and time again in boxing, pitted herself against others bigger and stronger who had done damage. She knew what it was like to take her body to new heights, new lows.

But never this. Never like this. She didn't have the vocabulary for any of it, and quite unfortunately felt a bit of an ache, knowing that it could not stand. It was just a rest, a holiday, a little blip in her otherwise hardscrabble life.

So enjoy it while you can, a little voice urged her.

And she decided to do just that.

CHAPTER TEN

ZERVOU LAID IN his bed, staring at his ceiling, while Ariadne slept in his arms. He had not slept a wink. Even as the morning light began to filter into the windows of the room, he was wide awake.

It was all very disorienting. This was not something he did. And getting rid of a woman after a healthy, enjoyable evening together had always been like second nature. Not something that required thought or effort.

This required both and a decision on just…what he was doing.

He didn't mind crossing blurry lines. A fake relationship to lure her father into the light was not complicated by sex. If anything, it was a nice bonus. The moment he'd laid eyes on her, he'd admitted that the potential was there.

But a woman falling asleep in his arms was not part of that bonus. It was not something that had ever even tempted him before. He enjoyed women and their company but was always happy to see them go. Happy to get his mind and life back to whatever the plan was at hand.

Last night, he hadn't been able to force himself to rouse her. He'd spent far too long staring at the bruise on her ribs. The crooked line of her nose. The way her left hand—curled gently on top of his chest—was slightly puffier than the right—like it was swollen from landing blows.

He had watched her box, even if it had always been practice. He understood that the kind of athleticism she dealt with meant her body would be marred by the sheer physicality of what she did. Day in. Day out.

He could not seem to get a full handle on the actual mark of those things on her soft, beautiful skin. It was an impotent kind of rage that reminded him of childhood. Scrabbling by. Refusing that which he wanted. And then finally breaking through, finding ease in the world around him. All while everyone he loved refused any of it.

It was a feeling, a concern, a complication he would have walked away from any other time, no matter how alluring the woman, because he had plans to enact. Revenge to seek.

But he could not walk away from Ariadne. Not when she was at the center of that revenge he sought.

Yes, that's the only reason you don't want to walk away.

Ariadne shifted in his arms, clearly awakened by the tension that had crept into the muscles that held her still. She yawned, blinked her eyes open. For a moment, their foggy brown depths met his, and all the discomfort swirling inside of him eased into something…else. Something he had no vocabulary for and probably wouldn't like it if he did.

Then she looked away from him. "Oh," she said, sitting up and—unfortunately—pulling the sheet up to cover her. She ran a free hand through her tangle of curls as she looked out the window. "Morning." She did not say this in greeting, more in observation of the time of day.

"Yes, it is morning, Ariadne. Early, though. Your first class is not until eight, correct?"

She made an agreeable kind of noise, still clutching the sheet to her chest, her gaze still on the windows.

"I will have breakfast brought up. And some more suitable clothes for your day."

She made a sound, kind of like a sigh. "You should call me Ari. I suppose we are…friends, after a fashion." She studied the discarded dress, then pulled the sheet off him and wrapped it around her as she got to her feet.

Ari. Friends. None of these things quite added up.

So he did not react to her words. Instead, he changed the subject. Next steps. "We will be going to Paris in a few days. A party that will garner more press than we've seen so far."

"Paris." She sighed a little. "How long?"

As though he was asking her to dig trenches in the arctic. "At least four days, I should think," he gritted out. "I'm quite sure I can find you training facilities should that really be necessary."

Her expression was neither grateful nor happy. She looked put upon.

He had to breathe through the anger trying to sneak into all the cracks of his persona. Because even if he had enjoyed last night, it was just a persona. Ariadne…*Ari*… was just a tool to get what he wanted.

Whether she appreciated his help or not was no matter. What was important this morning, though, was to make it clear that her sleeping in his bed was not something to confuse the matter.

How she accepted or didn't accept his help was of no matter, because at the end of this, *she* would be no matter. And because he was a good enough man, he thought it only fair to warn her, lest she get ideas.

"I do not need to reiterate to you that this is not…real."

She turned slowly. She stared at him, as if the words didn't penetrate. As if they were some kind of surprise. He expected hurt or anger. Something negative. But instead, she did the most confounding thing he'd ever seen.

She threw her head back and laughed.

"I do not see what is so funny."

But she just kept laughing as she disappeared into the bathroom.

He scowled after her. Then tossed the blanket off him, jerking on the discarded boxers and ignoring the rest. He would need a shower and quite a few cups of coffee to get his head on straight.

He texted instructions to his staff as he walked across the hall to the guest bath, since she was in his. When he was done with his shower, a mug of steaming coffee waited for him in the adjoining room.

He sipped it, not sure how he had ended up in the guest room and not his own. Still, when he stepped back into his own, the staff had set out breakfast on the patio as he'd instructed.

He poured himself another cup of coffee and drank it looking out over Corfu. Except he didn't see the buildings or the sea. He was thinking of last night.

He could not get a handle on this strange phenomenon. He was not used to physical pleasure lingering, twining with other feelings he could not parse. He was certainly not used to women *laughing* at him—in or out of the bedroom.

Ariadne—Ari—prompted so many different feelings he was struggling to find the right compartment for them all. Some were familiar: his frustration any time she seemed put upon by his offers of help. After all, he'd lived with that all his life. Sexual chemistry was also no stranger. He had been attracted to many a woman, acted on it in whatever ways he desired.

It was just this underlayer of something else.

Perhaps it all stemmed from the fact that there were some things she accepted from him without that put-upon air. She hadn't complained about the clothes or the meals. And really, he supposed, with the trips her only complaint was related to work, not being too proud to take help.

He could deal with that. He could even understand it. She was very dedicated to her work.

He thought of the bruise on her rib and tried not to scowl. Who in their right mind dedicated themselves to pain?

She stepped out onto the patio. Her damp hair was carefully braided tightly to her scalp. She wore athletic shorts and an overlarge T-shirt. Her feet were bare, her jewelry gone—no doubt since she was going to the boxing gym soon to handle her morning class.

She surveyed the table he sat at. "Oh, is breakfast real?" she asked, feigned innocence in the raise of her eyebrows.

He scowled at her, despite a glimmer of humor at her impertinence. "It is an important distinction, *glikí mou.*

You would not be the first woman to misunderstand a situation."

She lowered herself into the chair opposite him. "Perhaps the common denominator is not a woman's misunderstanding but you."

For a moment, he simply couldn't think. There were no retorts in his mouth. Nothing in his brain.

Perhaps the common denominator is you.

Ridiculous.

She sighed, the sound overly content as she put an arrangement of food on her plate. Not as much as he'd like to see her eat—choosing fruits and yogurts over the more decadent pastries—but again, she had a commitment to her profession. She was feeding an athlete's body.

Like the morning in Mykonos, she did not take any coffee or juice. Just drank ice water. He wished to see her glut herself on everything at this table and even opened his mouth to say so, but her *perhaps the common denominator is you* stopped him.

He was no one's common denominator. He drank his coffee and ate a piece of *bougatsa* as if in protest of her choices.

She hummed happily to herself as she ate and watched the sun finish its rise above the sea.

"This is like a totally different Corfu," she said thoughtfully, as if she didn't have a care in the world. "Quiet. Clean. Beautiful."

"Yes, perhaps you should stay here for the foreseeable future."

Wariness crept into her gaze, the way she held her shoulders. A little tighter. "Stay here?" she said, not looking at him.

"A next step in our little playacting."

"Stay here for the optics, but I would have my own room, yes?" She moved her gaze to his. Direct. Intent. But for a flicker of a moment, he thought he saw that careful mask of hers slip.

The question, the slight hesitation and that tension still in her shoulders did something to ease some of his frustrations. She may have laughed at him, but she was not quite so flippant about last night.

"If that is what you require." He smiled at her over his coffee. "But, of course, my bed is always open."

She made a vague kind of noise, her gaze going back out to sea. She didn't finish the yogurt on her plate, and this bothered him. Didn't an athlete's body need fuel? "I have to get to my first class. I don't suppose your Lurch is about to drive me?"

He rose. "I will drive you."

"Are you certain that is wise? Why, we've just spent the night together. Shouldn't you make sure to put some distance between us so I don't misunderstand?" She batted her eyelashes at him.

Teasing him.

He did not know what to do with it. No one teased him. No one had ever dared tease him. Perhaps when he'd been young and it had been mean-spirited, but those boys had paid.

She was not being mean-spirited, though, so he did not know what to do with this. It was something lighter, more familiar.

She sighed, stood and then patted his chest like he was a challenging puppy she was trying to train.

He was so agog, he simply took it.

"You need not concern yourself with me. I have no hopes for the future. From you or anyone else. I am considering this revenge plot nothing but a vacation from my real life on the way to making my father suffer for once. Trust me, Zervou, a woman in my position can't afford foolish daydreams. And I never take risks I can't afford."

He should be happy with that. Relieved. Instead he felt something like…sad.

For her.

Ari tried not to be uncomfortable when one of the guys who worked at the gym saw Zervou drop her off. They'd seen her leave with him. They'd seen him come into the gym twice now.

Besides, that was the whole ruse. Let people know they were together. God knew the men who worked here likely had more of a gossip network back to her father than the high society restaurants and resorts Zervou frequented.

So she pretended today was no different than any other. Zervou's…presence was about to be very common. If she stayed at his estate for the next few weeks, working up to an engagement announcement, he might have to drive her around quite a bit or have someone else do it. She had never had the option to learn how to drive.

She still wasn't sure how she felt about staying at his estate. Did she insist in a separate room, call last night a one-off? Insist once was good and enough. Just the taste she needed to know what sex was like, and that was quite enough.

Or did she give in to what her body wanted? More of *that*. Because last night had most certainly not been enough. It seemed like seeing just a small crack of light. She wanted to throw the door open and see the whole tableau.

But she knew too much of something that amazing could be the start of an addiction. One that would hurt to break. Ruin her to break.

No, she would not be ruined.

She went to the locker room to ensure all the things she'd left behind yesterday were still in her locker. She got ready and tried to put all thoughts of what happened after her work away.

She taught her first class. It was one of her favorites. A smattering of angry teenagers as she'd once been, either happy to spend their summer mornings learning how to fight or sent here by well-meaning adults.

The boys were always trying prove some kind of dominance over her, and she enjoyed proving them wrong at every turn. Not just a personal satisfaction, but a hope it would be a lifelong lesson that *might* did not always get them what they wanted.

The one girl she had in the class was always trying to earn Ari's approval, so Ari had to be careful not to give it all the time, though she wanted to. What the girl lacked in muscle and substance she made up for in determination and attitude.

After class, she had some training of her own, followed by an intense workout. After her too-large breakfast this morning, she'd need to ensure she gave her all in both.

But before she could move into her cardio plans for the morning, she was summoned into her manager's office.

Lefteris owned the gym, and though he had been initially skeptical about her back when she'd been a teenager brought by her dedicated teacher, he'd since become her staunchest supporter. A support she believed in the most because she'd had to earn it.

She didn't know why he would call her in today, unless there was some kind of issue with her upcoming fight.

The fact that didn't cause her any worry had her chewing on her bottom lip as she walked toward his office. She should be devastated at the possibility something might go wrong with the fight. Her life was a series of fight, everything else revolving around those perfect moments of letting her body *fight*.

But a strange sense of relief tried to worm its way through her. Like she was…tired. Burnt out.

But that couldn't be possible, so she shook that odd feeling away and knocked on Lefteris's door. At the gruff "come in," she entered.

He looked up from his laptop—old and whirring so loudly she could hear it at the doorway—and nodded. "Sit, Ari."

She did as she was told, taking the seat across from his worn desk, folding her hands in her lap. "I hope all is well with the fight."

"Yes. You seem ready."

"I am," she said firmly, because she was. She worked hard. Every day she worked hard to be ready.

"Good. That isn't what I called you in to discuss." He turned his ancient laptop to face her. On the screen was a picture. Ari leaned forward to study it.

Grainy and poor quality but still faces could be made out. Her face—eyes closed, chin tipped up as she leaned back into Zervou, who had his arm around her abdomen. Intimately.

So intimately, she'd somehow thought it a good idea to go home with him. Have sex with him.

She should probably have regrets, but even after his *this is not real* proclamation, she had none. The night had been…amazing. Truly. As an athlete, she thought she knew everything her body could do. She'd learned new things last night.

And now was not the time to consider them. She shifted, cleared her throat. "Is there a problem?"

"No," Lefteris replied. "Problem is not the word. Opportunity, I think, is a better one."

Confused, Ari said nothing.

"There was talk, of course, since he has now been here twice. And word is he dropped you off this morning. But I still did not believe it. Until this. You…and Zervou Kritikos."

Ari tried not to fidget in her seat. She didn't know why they'd be discussing this, and she could hardly tell Lefteris it was fake… Well, sort of fake. So all she could do was confirm. "Yes."

"I do not wish to dig into your private business, Ari. But it has to be said. If you could talk to him about sponsoring you, we could go to the fight in Minsk. If you put a bug in his ear, we could host fights in his new stadium. Do you understand what a boon it would be for our gym if *Zervou Kritikos* was behind us?"

Ari knew he was right, but it twisted a lot of discomfort in her chest. She couldn't blame Lefteris for such a thought, but to bring it to her… To suggest…

"Are you suggesting I prostitute myself for the gym, Lefteris?"

The older man sighed. "I have been nothing but good to you, Ari."

Which did not answer her direct question, did it? Still, he wasn't wrong. Not everyone had been kind to her here. Not everyone had been supportive. But ever since seeing her first bout, really seeing her potential, Lefteris had been both. A manager in many senses of the word. She would not be where she was without his help.

Now he wanted her to beg for money. From Zervou. Mr. This Isn't Real.

As if she could ever believe something so glorious was hers to have and hold. He didn't know her at all, did he? And didn't need to. That was the point he was making, after all. They could have fun on the side of their mission, but it didn't change that they would part cleanly. As strangers.

And there was nothing sad about that.

But Lefteris wanted her to use her nonexistent romantic influence on Zervou and…

Real didn't matter. Not in this instance. She would not beg for money. She'd worked too hard and come too far to owe anyone.

Even Zervou.

Everything he offered had to be his own idea, or she would not take it. It was a line she had to draw for herself to keep this whole bizarre situation from getting out of control. From turning into something it would be hard to lose.

Asking and getting could be an addiction like any

other, and Ari knew when to not allow herself luxuries that might become too enticing.

Do you?

She pushed that traitorous thought away. Yes, she was enjoying something now, but she understood it was temporary, and it was only because they were simply reaching for the same goal—the end of her father. If Zervou was mixed up in her profession, that could lead to messy and complex situations after Erjon was taking care of.

No, she wouldn't risk that.

But how did she explain that to her manager, who thought she really was in a relationship with Zervou?

"Lefteris, I'm sorry. I do not feel comfortable asking for money from the man I'm seeing at this time. I suppose if he offered of his own accord, I would not shut him down. I would send him to come discuss it with you. But I cannot… I have to have some integrity."

"I could ask—"

"No," Ari said firmly, getting to her feet. The thought of anyone going to Zervou on her behalf and asking made her feel a kind of shame she didn't fully understand and didn't want to. "I need you to let this be. To go on with my fights, my opportunities as we always have. It is important to me."

He scowled. "Integrity doesn't always pay off, Ari. In fact, it often does the opposite."

Ari thought that over. She couldn't argue with it. God knew, she might be in a better position if she had a little less integrity. She could have gotten herself involved in whatever criminal activity her father was wrapped up in that gave him money and power and influence, even if he had to scuttle behind closed doors and alleys and whatever hiding spots he currently resided in.

But she would not be her father.

"I have scrabbled. I have struggled. But I have maintained who I am at many a cost. If I lose that, I have nothing. I am nothing. So, no. I will not risk what no one can take from me."

He grunted, acquiescing even if he wasn't happy about it.

Relief swamped her, making her muscles feel shaky. Still, she rose. Still, she told him what she needed to. "I will be away next week. You will have to have Daphne take my classes. She's ready, and it will be good for her to have some practice without me looking over her shoulder."

"You have a fight in two weeks," Lefteris said, studying her with narrowed eyes. As if, just by looking at her, he could tell whether being away would jeopardize that.

"Yes, I will maintain my own training while I'm away. You know I do not like to lose."

Again, he made a grunting sound, then leaned forward with that same narrowed-eyed gaze. "You aren't planning on quitting, are you? Retiring to settle down and what not?"

Ari snorted, even as something like panic bumped around in her chest. Quit? And then who would she be? "Don't be ridiculous."

But Lefteris only made a dismissive kind of noise and waved her away.

She left the office, tension in her shoulders. Quit? Retire? What would she do without boxing? It was almost unfathomable…

Almost.

Because if she walked away from this fake relationship with Zervou with a decent amount of money…was retiring a possibility? She'd never even considered it before now, but Lefteris had put it in her head. Did she want that possibility?

The terrible thing was…she didn't know.

CHAPTER ELEVEN

ZERVOU SPENT HIS DAY working on the Erjon dilemma. Where was the weasel? He should at least be sending someone traceable to watch Ariadne by now.

Ari.

Friends.

His mind kept returning to that one crystalized moment. Her, wrapped in a sheet, calling them friends *after a fashion*. The morning light burnishing her skin gold.

Such a small moment. Such a nothing moment. And yet it lodged there like the root of a weed—he could not pull it out completely, so it just stuck there, deep in the recesses of his mind.

And he didn't know what to do with it, because it wasn't a problem to be solved. It was simply a moment. What did one do with a moment?

It wasn't like his father dying in front of him. Not like his mother's wails as the life drained out of the man she loved. No, even though those were moments he'd never quite eradicated from his mind, they had come with action items. When people died, there were things to do.

When a woman simply asked him to call her by a shortened name, called them friends *after a fashion*, there was nothing to do.

Except hunt down her father. Lure him out into the light so he could spend the rest of his life in jail. Then Zervou and *Ari* could go their separate ways and whatever this strange…blip was could go with her. Whether she accepted all his help with a positive attitude or that wary distrust, she would still leave him better than she'd been. She would not be able to deny or negate his help.

And *that* was a positive.

A knock sounded on his office door, and when he offered a "come in," Bacchus entered.

"The Paris arrangements have all been made. We have found a rental just outside the city with the required amenities."

Meaning, a gym from which Ari could do her boxing and whatever other kind of training she desired.

"The plane is ready to leave in the morning," Bacchus continued. "I will accompany you, but I plan to leave Sebastian behind to continue to lookout for signs of Hyseni if you agree."

Sebastian ran the Kritikos security for the most part, though everything went through Bacchus, security included.

Zervou tapped his fingers on his desk. It was a good plan. More than likely, Erjon would poke around Corfu or send someone at his behest while they were gone.

It would be a start. It would have to be a start.

"Very well. As for today, I will need you to pick up Ms. Malis at the gym at five this evening," Zervou told him. Though he was tempted to handle the errand himself, he thought it wise to give them yet a little distance. Perhaps she had laughed at the idea that sex last night might be more, but he wanted to ensure she understood.

He had no desire to leave anyone heartbroken, and she was the more vulnerable party here, no matter what she thought.

He had to protect her from herself.

"Yes, sir."

"Get there a little early. Watch the comings and goings. If someone from Erjon's camp is watching her, it's likely to be there, where they might think she's not being protected or watched. I want a sign of him before we go to Paris. I want to know he has noticed what's going on."

"Yes, sir."

Some rumbling. Some inkling. His plan had to work. And he needed a sign it was. *Now.*

Zervou sent Bacchus on his way, then made a few calls to check the progress on the stadium. Much was left to be done, but he already had some sporting vendors interested. Eager.

Football, basketball, volleyball. Some wrestling had been discussed. He had not had any meetings with boxing agencies, but his interest was certainly piqued now. Ari's boxing gym boasted nothing impressive—except her—so he wasn't sure he wanted to dabble there just yet.

But he thought of watching her just practice. How mesmerizing it all was. With the right marketing, a boxing match could no doubt be a draw. Especially with Ari as the star.

Still, he set that aside for the time being. He had to ensure his Paris trip was a success. He had a man to destroy before he worried about his own successes.

A few hours later, when a call from Bacchus came through his personal cell, Zervou did not know whether to feel victorious or trepidation. A direct call could only mean something had happened.

"Is everything well?"

"Yes, sir. Ms. Malis is getting ready to leave, but I thought you should know. There is a man here loitering outside the boxing gym. I have sent his photograph to Sebastian to be sure, but I believe he is a man from the Petrov family."

The family Erjon had worked for when he'd murdered Zervou's father. There had not been a connection there in some time. Zervou had taken care most of the Petrovs himself. He had certainly undercut any power they had as a crime family.

But Erjon had always been his main target. And now what scraps were left of the Petrov family were poking around Erjon's daughter? Now that she had a connection to Zervou?

It had to be the hint of something he'd been hoping for. No doubt Erjon *and* the Petrovs would scuttle back into partnership in the bowels of wherever they were hiding from his considerable reach.

"I would like you to go inside the gym and fetch Ari…adne yourself. Make sure this man knows she is protected without necessarily letting on that you recognize him or see him as a threat. Just make it clear to anyone who might be watching that Ariadne has protection."

"Yes, sir."

"Then put Sebastian on finding any current link between Hyseni and the Petrovs. I want to know every member of the Petrov family still alive and not in jail—and where they're hiding."

"Already on it."

"Excellent." And it was. Because it was a sign. His plan was working. There was still time to tease it out, but the beginnings had started.

And Paris would be the next step.

Paris. Ari couldn't believe she was in Paris. Literally every other thought in her mind drifted away as they drove through the city.

She had left Greece. She was in a foreign country seeing things she had never even dreamed of seeing. Even her wildest fantasies didn't include Paris.

She'd told that to Zervou on the plane.

He'd told her she needed better fantasies.

Perhaps she did.

Ari hadn't told her mother that they were traveling when she'd talked to her last night. She had just listened to her mother's progress. Mostly positive, though Maria was already making noises about being *all cured* and ready to be released.

Her counselors did not agree. So, Mother stayed. Something she did without argument only because she felt guilty, Ari knew.

She'd set her worry aside then, and she set it aside now. She was in Paris. She wanted to focus on that, revel in that.

Still her mind lingered on last night. After she'd hung up with her mother, Zervou had served her dessert. He didn't say it was meant to be any kind of pick-me-up, but the timing was suspicious. Like he wanted to comfort her in some way.

Maybe that was why she had, yet again, spent the night in his bed.

She hadn't meant to. She thought there should be some care taken to make sure she didn't develop a habit that couldn't been broken.

Sex felt like a dangerous precipice. There was the high of it, the desperation of it. The way those feelings lingered and never seemed to fully disappear. Because even in this car, with Paris all around them, she only needed to think about last night to feel her cheeks warm and her stomach clench.

How could this be different than desiring a drink, one more roll of the dice?

No, she had to be more careful. Stronger.

When the car pulled to a stop, Ari could only stare at the building out the window. It wasn't a hotel or even an apartment. It was a full-on house, except house wasn't the right word. An *estate* like what he had in Corfu. Perhaps a little smaller but just as beautiful.

Trees and flowers and greenery overflowed along the drive and around the entry to the building. It gleamed, windows sparkling, the soft French light making it all seem like some kind of fairy tale.

"Well, this is something," she managed to say when Zervou came to her side of the car and opened the door, then helped her out into the warm afternoon. She could hear birds chirping and the rustle of the breeze in the trees. There was something spicy in the air.

Maybe she was dreaming.

"Just you wait," he said, clearly pleased with himself and the mansion he was leading her to.

Up the white stairs. The front door opened, staff already welcoming them inside.

"I want to show you something before we take a rest

before dinner," he said, guiding her with her arm tucked in his.

She followed, speechless. Gigantic paintings dominated huge white walls… Beautiful views from every towering window, even as he led her down a set of stairs into what couldn't possibly be called a basement. It was too big, too nice, too grand.

He opened a door, drew her into a large room and flipped on the lights.

She surveyed her surroundings in utter shock.

"It should be everything you need to stay for as long as we like," Zervou said proudly.

It was. More than she'd come to expect, even from him. It was a fully equipped gym with a boxing ring at the center. Everything was newer and nicer than anything at her home gym.

She took a few steps toward the boxing ring. It shouldn't be amazing. He was rich. But this was…more than she'd expected. She wouldn't have to fight to have the time and place to train. It was all right here.

It did something to her lungs. Squeezed them tight. Discomfort and excitement twined into a feeling she didn't recognize, didn't want. It was too weighty and complicated.

Because she wanted this and knew she shouldn't. She trusted him not to use it like a lure, and she shouldn't.

She was *moved* and shouldn't be.

Grow some spine, Ari. She tried. Tried so hard to harden a shell around a strangely soft heart as she turned to face him. She could not offer gratitude, though she should. Gratitude could be used against her, and she had to be unaffected. By this. By him.

"I will need a sparring partner," she said, tossing her hair back behind her shoulder. "I don't suppose you scrounged up one of those."

He studied her with those dark eyes. There was a spark of something that had her chest aching, and yet she couldn't name it. Understand it. She certainly hadn't hurt his feelings. This meant nothing to him. He had made it clear *she* meant nothing to him beyond revenge and some pleasure in the bedroom.

"I can act as your sparring partner," he said, with a slight curve of his mouth that made it seem like an offer for a lot more than sparring.

Still, she pretended to take him at face value, to protect herself in a moment of feeling off balance.

She eyed him skeptically. He had the body for it, even if the exquisite clothes didn't make it look so in the moment. But she had felt every inch of that body, under her hands, over her skin. Yes, he could no doubt handle the simple act of boxing.

But he didn't have her knowledge or skill.

"Are you worried that I might actually be able to hold my own?" he asked, one eyebrow raised in challenge. "Are you *afraid*, Ari?"

She rolled her eyes dramatically. "Many an arrogant man has received a jab to the face thinking he was better than a woman."

"I have no doubts you are the better boxer, *glikí mou*, but I know how to hold my own." He gestured toward the ring. "It is only practice. I have seen you pull punches in practice. What is the harm?"

"I pull those punches, yes, but they still land."

"Then I'll ask you not to break my nose. Or do I need to beg?"

For a moment, her brain fractured—from the insult of using him as a sparring partner to the idea of him begging for anything.

It brought to mind the way he'd knelt before her that first night. What he'd said about her belly button ring. That dangerous flicker of passion began to sputter to life when she'd told herself she wouldn't go looking for this.

She had to be careful. Addiction to anything so good would be ruinous.

So she stepped away from him and pretended to survey the boxing ring. She considered her clothes. The travel set was casual, a little loose for actual boxing. But they weren't *boxing*. They were… She wasn't sure. One of them was trying to prove a point, probably. She just wasn't fully sure *who*.

As long as she won, though, she didn't have to worry about what kind of point. So she moved for the ring.

There was a shelf of gloves and wraps and punch mitts just outside it. Ari took her time selecting what she wanted, then climbed into the ring without looking at him again.

She walked across the mat, tested the give. Since she was wearing sandals, she tossed them off to the side. She turned to face him.

He'd also taken off his shoes. They stood facing each other from their separate corners, and Ari couldn't seem to stop a laugh from bubbling out from her. "This is ridiculous."

His mouth quirked, but he shrugged rather than agreed. "Humor me."

He crossed to the center, so she did, too, then frowned when she saw that he'd chosen mitts over gloves.

"You should wear gloves, not just those pads. You can hit me back. I can take it."

"No," he said, with no further explanation. "Let's just see if you can land one around me blocking with the mitts."

Again, she rolled her eyes. Of course she could land *one*. He was bigger and just as strong, and he might be faster, though she wasn't fully convinced of that. But her *life* was boxing. If she couldn't land a punch on a random man—no matter how good of shape he was in—she shouldn't be in a boxing ring.

She sighed. "Fine." She started moving back and forth on the balls of her feet, enjoying the feel of the mat beneath her bare feet, the clean gloves on her hands. All so familiar.

Except facing a man with intense dark eyes and an expression she couldn't read. She started easy. A jab, one at a time with a break between.

He blocked the pulled punches with his mitts, as she'd expected.

Slowly, over time, she worked up to sequences, still keeping her full power locked. She bobbed, she weaved, and she didn't go for the blow. She could have. Many times. But she couldn't seem to bring herself to do it. Even a pulled punch would hurt, could leave a mark.

He was always so perfectly put together. What would an imperfection do to that perfect face?

"Come on then," he said, a flicker of irritation in him now. "Show me what you're really made of."

She could have. She saw the pattern—his and her

own. If she jabbed with her right, and he blocked with his right, his left hand fell just enough she could have gotten a solid uppercut in.

But she did not take the opportunity.

He had not put on gloves. He would not hit her—even at her invitation. It was a kind of, well, integrity to choose that. To refuse, so instantly and flatly, to return a blow, even in practice.

Perhaps she didn't have to appreciate it, but she could admire it. And it could undermine her desire to land any kind of blows upon him.

So she went for the clinch, with the thought if she pushed him back to the ropes, she could call it a win without actually hitting him.

She managed to get him close to the ropes. She could have landed a few jabs. She could have done a lot of things, but she could not bring herself to even *kind of* hurt this man. She didn't understand why. What it meant. Who she was in this strange world of Paris and delicious meals and lovely clothes and…

Him.

He flipped it around in a quick, easy move. Not a boxing move at all. No, it spoke more to some kind of ground fighting. She faced the ropes, he was behind her now, his arms wrapped around hers so that hers were trapped at her sides.

She was breathing heavily from the exertion of bouncing around and from holding herself back. From whatever was assaulting her mind. This strange, confusing waterfall of feelings and doubts—in herself, in her choices, in *everything.*

Except him.

"That isn't a boxing move," she told him, breathless and probably not from exertion.

He didn't address that accusation. "Are you losing on purpose, Ari?"

She could feel the long, hard weight of him. The rumble of his voice in her ear. The press and pull of his chest moving against her back. It all shivered through her, sensation and need. But more so when he said *Ari*.

She had told him to call her that, since no one aside from him used her full name, but here in the moment it had a weight she could not really wade through.

Mostly because all she wanted was to feel him moving inside of her.

"I have never thrown a fight in my life," she shot back at him, frustrated and emotional in ways she did not understand.

"But this wasn't a fight, was it?" he said, still low and in her ear. Accusatory. But the accusation felt deeper than words.

All of this felt *deeper* than what they were actually saying, and she hated it. So she strove for some kind of flippancy in her return.

"Would you have rather I bloodied your lip?" she demanded.

She felt his sigh against her cheek. "Perhaps."

She didn't know why that had her eyes prickling with tears. Perhaps because it spoke to something deeper inside herself. She would rather feel unencumbered by the idea of landing a blow. She would rather not feel this restless, pounding need inside of her every time he was near.

But she could not be smart enough to eradicate it in any way except one.

"Touch me, Zervou."

A sound rumbled through him that then rumbled through her. It seemed to touch nerve endings all along her skin, this sound.

"Ask nicely, *glikí mou*," he murmured, sliding his mouth down her neck.

Somewhere in the back of her mind, she thought she should be offended. Should hold onto some kind of pride. Why should she ask for anything?

But the "please" was out of her mouth before that dim thought had a chance to take root. She wanted his touch more than she wanted her pride.

It should be a terrifying prospect. It should feel wrong.

It didn't.

His hands loosened at her sides so that she could free her arms, but she didn't. Not really. She let them hang there as she leaned back against him, his clever mouth doing arousing things to her neck as his hands moved under her shirt, found the bare skin there. He traced muscle and bone, unclasped her bra with nimble fingers, then pulled both items of clothing from her body.

She arched into him, into his touch. Fingers brushed taut nipples, teeth scraped against the curve of her shoulder. Physical pleasure after wave of physical pleasure… That coiling rush of need…

It made no more sense than her whirling feelings, but it was concrete. He would take her up peak after peak, and there would be a conclusion. Simple. Straightforward.

He tugged the loose pants from her, and they fell easily to her feet. Her underwear were next, until she was once again naked, with him fully clothed behind her. What did that say about them?

Didn't matter. All that mattered was that he touched her where she throbbed in desperate anticipation. "Zer—"

He turned her to face him in a rough move, his eyes blazing. His breath heaving nearly as much as hers was. But it was the direct gaze that had her heart tripping over itself. Had her wishing she was stronger, smarter, something.

But she was none of those things. Not when his mouth crushed to hers. Then she was only his.

He lowered her to the ground, the give of the mat beneath her, the hard, hot weight of him above her. He slid his hands over her arms, arranging them over her head, then clasping her wrists together with just one of his hands.

She knew moves that could knock him off, and she had no doubt he would get up if she asked. If she demanded.

This was not force. It was something else entirely.

And it required her acceptance as much as his. His understanding as much as hers. She had been coming to grips with trusting a man she shouldn't, but she had allowed him to believe she was still skeptical.

Now he must know. Now he must see.

And still she did not try to buck him off. She did not tell him to stop when he sheathed himself in a condom. She arched her body to his and moaned in time with him as they joined.

It was an explosion that eviscerated foundations. That tangled up and crossed all her carefully placed wires. Wild, restless, desperate. Different than other times before, like they were fighting each other in the midst of all this erotic pleasure.

She shuddered through one climax and then the next, sobbing out his name, his grip on her wrists never loosening. She never wanted it to.

"Ari." His voice was rough, fierce. "Look at me."

She blinked her eyes open to meet his gaze, held it as he slowed, driving her up into something else. Not a fight this time. No... But she only knew of fights and survival, so she didn't know what this was.

Except too much. Too big. Her heart felt like bursting and tears pricked her eyes, but she still couldn't look away from the dark depths of his. Even as the crash came over her, and he thrust deep into her one last time, growling out his own climax, they held each other's gaze.

For ticking moments after. As if they both had the same question echoing unanswerable in their heads.

What *was* that?

Pinned beneath him, the waves of pleasure slowly ebbing out as her breathing began to even enough to realize his was in the same state hers was, and that did nothing to steady her or make her feel better.

If they were both upended, how would they survive this?

She closed her eyes on a wave of emotional pain. What was she doing? She knew better. She'd always had to know better. She was letting a soft life make her soft when that would only lead to her own doom. Perhaps his, too, but he was a man. A rich man. He would survive.

What would she do?

He finally released her wrists. Carefully, balancing

his weight, he moved off her and got to his feet. He held out a hand to help her up.

For a moment, she could only stare at the offered hand. Her brain wasn't functioning. Everything inside of her was jumbled.

"Come. Let us get ready for dinner." His voice was little more than a rasp, belying the simply words.

What had happened wasn't simple, for either of them.

But. Dinner. Yes. They had…plans. And that was just…sex. They had done it before. They'd likely do it again. It wasn't different. She had to determine it could *not* be different.

But when he helped her to her feet, he did not meet her gaze, and she did not meet his, and everything that had once felt easy no longer did.

CHAPTER TWELVE

DINNER WAS STILTED. They went their separate ways after. Zervou buried himself in work the next day—Ari in training by herself.

Zervou felt distracted and restless, but there were no other options here. He had work, plans. She did, too. Whatever that moment had been yesterday…it was nothing. And tonight, they had a group of partygoers to convince they were seconds away from becoming engaged.

No matter what he told himself, though, he didn't feel like himself. Perhaps he was coming down with something.

Still, he got ready for the party, reminding himself of the plan. Show up, not just with Ari but never take his eyes off her. Drop hints about an upcoming engagement. Turn the screws on Erjon. Make him pressured into making a move.

Zervou felt more settled in that, more sure. Determined.

And then Ariadne appeared, ready to leave for the party.

The gown was white. It draped over one shoulder, leaving the other bare. The fabric nipped in at the waist, skimmed her hips. Her hair had been left curly and loose, and gold winked up her ears and around her neck.

She was a vision, and for too many moments, that was it. The vision of her and this strange riot inside of him.

She looked like a bride.

Something inside his chest clutched once before he iced it away, reminding himself who he was and that her beauty suited his purposes. And meant absolutely nothing else.

He did not meet her gaze—or maybe she did not meet his. They exchanged no pleasantries, simply left the estate and headed for his car. Bacchus drove them into the city and the party that would be full of socialites, royalty and the like. Ari's face and name would be splashed across all media, linked with his.

The satisfaction he had over that came from knowing Erjon would see it.

He told himself this. Repeatedly.

Inside the party, there were people watching, talking. He'd seen more than one intrepid young person sneak a photo or video from their phones. He would need to dance with Ari at least once to get the appropriate photographs circulating.

At the moment, they were in an ancient ballroom all gilded gold and bright. It nearly gave him a headache, all this wealth on display. Ari in the middle of it.

She had been swept away by a small group of women who were asking her all sorts of questions about her boxing. She was handling them well enough, enough Zervou had felt comfortable letting her be swept away from him for a time. But right now, he couldn't seem to occupy himself in any other way other than to watch her from where he stood on the other side of the dancing.

He wondered why he'd thought to dress her in white. The color of the gown made her skin seem like gold in candlelight. It seemed to add a richness to the sable curls and dark eyes. The gold in her ears glittered, and he could momentarily distract himself by questioning whether or not her bellybutton ring was being worn under all that white silk.

But then he would think of the boxing ring.

She had frustrated him, not willing to land any blow—real or otherwise. At first he had been offended. Perhaps felt as though his manhood was being impinged. She may be a boxer, but he'd grown up on the streets and scrabbled for everything he had. He could take a damn punch.

But then he'd come to a worse realization, because he'd seen it in her face. This was not arrogance. She just didn't want to cause him pain. Which spoke to something…soft.

She couldn't afford soft. And he wanted nothing to do with it.

His phone chimed from deep in his pocket. Normally he would not answer in such a situation, but he'd set his phone for only Bacchus to get through, and if Bacchus was contacting him, it was important.

He pulled the phone out of his pocket, read the text message.

We have traced the Petrov to Athens. He met with a man—not Hyseni—whom we will look further into.

Athens. Promising. Zervou had long believed Erjon had found a hiding place on the outskirts of Athens or

Svilengrad or both. That had been a hunch he'd never been able to prove, but the Petrov spy meeting with someone in Athens was certainly interesting.

Steps. Steps toward everything he wanted. *Finally.*

He glanced at Ari. They would need to dance. They needed some photo ops. Now was the time.

He crossed the dance floor, made a beeline for her. He didn't bother to look at the women talking to Ari. He only had eyes for her. A ruse. of course.

"You will have to excuse me. I would like to dance with my… Excuse us." He'd said it on purpose. The *my...* and then let it trail off. Stir up questions and glances.

The engagement would be sooner rather than later, and he wanted some speculation surrounding it. He wanted Erjon infuriated enough to make a mistake, to stop using his lackeys.

He pulled her into his arms and ignored the sudden tightness in his own skin.

"Is everything all right?" she asked him, letting herself be led in the dance. "You look angry."

He tried to smooth out his expression. Of course he wasn't angry. He had next steps in their plan. He was… determined.

He swept her in a turn and ignored the punch of lust and feeling at the smell of her waving over him like a restful cloud.

"There has been someone keeping tabs on you," he told her, matter-of-fact. "A member of the Petrov family. A family your father worked with years ago. He was watching you back in Corfu at the gym, and since we left, he headed to Athens to meet with another unknown. It is a lead."

He could feel her gaze on his, but he kept his on the room around them.

"Years ago, as when he killed your father?" she asked softly.

He couldn't wonder at how easily she put together that connection, but still he stiffened against it. "Yes."

"And you did not eradicate them?"

Ah, she knew him well. "I undercut much of the Petrov family's influence. The main perpetrators are behind bars, and one was killed in some in-fighting during a raid. Perhaps they were who Erjon worked for, but he made the choice to kill my father in the shakedown. So he is my main target. Everyone else of import has been taken care of."

She was quiet for a few moments, and he dared a glance down at her. Her expression was pensive.

"If someone is keeping tabs on me," she said thoughtfully, "that means Erjon has sent someone to do his dirty work."

"Yes, perhaps more than one. But we are on the trail now. Erjon is eating up the crumbs we're leaving him. It is forward movement."

Ari nodded, then looked up at him. "Will you pull him out of hiding if he doesn't come himself?"

"I believe he won't be able to resist coming himself, but even if he doesn't do it of his own volition, we will drag him into the light."

"You would go on the attack without drawing him out?"

Zervou shrugged. Truth be told, his plans all seemed oddly nebulous now. But he knew the steps. He'd plotted them out before he'd even discovered Ari's existence. "It is not attack, per se. I have the evidence needed to put him away forever. The money to ensure justice is served regardless of the system. If we have to go into his lair and drag him out, it will be done. We only need to find him. And we are that much closer."

The song ended, and dessert was served in the grand dining room. They sat down, and Zervou forced himself to speak with a couple who had some questions about his holdings in Marseille. He put the businessman mask on. He did his duty.

Ari did not. She spent her time looking off in the distance. She toyed with her dessert without eating, and he didn't think this time it had anything to do with worry over her upcoming fight.

When some of the people had filtered away, and they were alone at their end of the table, he leaned toward her. Bystanders would see a couple sharing an intimate conversation. He supposed they wouldn't be wrong.

"What is on your mind?"

Her gaze moved from the window to her plate. She set down the fork. "It's strange. Ever since I was a teen, I dreamed of revenge, of retribution. But now that it is seemingly within reach, I wonder..."

"Wonder what?"

Her eyes lifted to his now. Her expression serious, perhaps...lost. She looked young and in need of direction. He had never seen that from her before. But her words weren't naive or youthful. They were more mature than anything he'd been thinking.

"What is on the other side of revenge? Of him finally seeing a jail cell? I try to picture it, feel some satisfaction, but it is just…blank. What changes if he's put away forever? What's different than the past decade?"

What if. Zervou did not like what-ifs. He did not like these feelings inside of him. So he made sure his mouth curved, even if it was more grimace than smile. "Second thoughts, Ari?"

"No, it isn't like that." She shook her head. "He deserves to rot in jail. It isn't so much about him. I'm just… thinking aloud. Beyond."

"Why should we think beyond our revenge?" he demanded, quietly but intensely. Revenge had been moving him forward for years. Revenge and taking care of what had been left in wreckage. What more could there be?

But now she'd introduced this strange, murky *after*. Where he would have avenged everything.

And still, his mother would not accept his help.

Ari would go on her way.

And then…what?

She sighed, sounding sad and lost again. "Why indeed," she murmured.

Leaving him feeling unmoored…because he didn't have an answer to his own question.

They stayed in Paris for five days. Zervou never once stepped foot in the room downstairs again. Ari trained during the day alone. They went to dinners and parties. Stories and pictures about them made their way around Europe. Engagement rumors swirled.

Without discussing it, they did not share a bed or anything more intimate than a quick kiss or embrace for the cameras. Everything they'd been went back to being very…businesslike.

A relief, really, Ari assured herself. Proof there was no addiction, no mistakes. Just enjoyment when it suited.

Even back in Corfu, in his grand estate, they managed to see very little of each other privately. And in public, it was always an act, a farce. With a strange new distance she didn't understand and did not want to.

What was not a relief was the persistent nagging feeling of…something changing. Shifting inside of her. This idea of something more or beyond when her entire life had been two things: survival most of all, and the hope to someday end her father.

Now, Mother was safe, at least for the time being. Ari was fed and more than well taken care of—again, momentarily. She still got to throw herself into the job she loved, which would last long beyond Zervou.

She knew all these things were fleeting, and still she could not picture a life with her father in jail, Zervou no longer here and going back to nothing but survival. She knew that was what was next, but…

Right now, she was happy. Not with everything but happier than she'd ever been. More settled. And it allowed her to see beyond revenge and survival. It allowed her to see herself and her life as a whole, not just day after day to struggle through.

And so she found herself asking questions she'd never had time to consider before.

What would it take to be happy? In the real life she had coming for her once this fake life was over?

Zervou appeared in her peripheral vision like an answer. When he could never be.

She lifted a glass of water to her lips and pretended not

to see him until he stepped up to the table on the patio. A glimmering Corfu morning spread out beyond him.

"Good morning," he offered.

They had existed as strangers since returning. She had half thought of trying to go back to her apartment just to see if he would notice.

But then she'd catch Bacchus out of her periphery vision at the gym. She was being watched or watched after, whichever way she wanted to view it. And since she wanted to have no conflict, she'd simply gone along with staying put.

But he'd made a habit of not seeking her out in the mornings. Letting her go to the gym and about her day before requiring her presence in the evening for whatever public event he had lined up.

So she tried not to shift or act uncomfortable with his appearance now, even if she was. "Good morning."

He said nothing else, but he placed a small jewelry box on the table next to her plate.

She stared at it, confused for a moment.

He didn't seem to have his usual patience this morning. "Open it," he ordered.

Frowning, she took the box and opened it. Only realizing it was a ring box when she saw the contents.

It was so beautiful. If she had thought of what a fake engagement ring from Zervou Kritikos would look like, she would have imagined something flashy. Something that would photograph well—big and loud. Beautiful, of course, but more show than substance.

Instead, the ring in this box was understated. Beautiful, ridiculously expensive no doubt, but it felt made for her.

•

And that was ridiculous.

"You will wear this at all times," he said, an order meant to be followed and a reminder this was all just part of the plan. The only reason she was even part of the plan was her bloodline she did not wish to recognize.

She looked at the sparkling gold, the pretty green jewel. She didn't even know what kind it was. Which was a reminder of *who* she was. "What about when I am boxing?"

He eyed her. She didn't meet his gaze, but she could feel it, his gaze and a tension inside of him that made little sense to her. And she did not wish it to make it make sense, because if she understood…

Having these lines drawn was her last defense against everything that had happened in that boxing ring in Paris. An unraveling she couldn't survive.

"I worry there is nowhere at the boxing gym safe enough to keep something as fine as this ring from getting stolen," she explained. "No matter how good and loyal people are, money is an enticing lure."

"You may leave it in the car then, with Bacchus or whomever drives you. But as much as possible, in public, it should be on your finger. We do not want any questions."

Questions. No, they didn't want that. They wanted Erjon. Though Zervou's men had followed the member of the Petrov family and the man he'd met in Athens and a few other meandering possibilities, they had yet to get any clarity on where Erjon himself might be.

This was supposed to draw him out. Fully. He would not allow her to be married off to the man who wished to destroy him. He would need to stop it.

“Put it on then,” Zervou directed.

She didn’t want to. Everything inside of her resisted reaching out for it, but he’d given a direction and as much as she was used to following her own directions and no one else’s, he existed in some other place for her, didn’t he?

She lifted the box, still resisting touching the actual ring. “This is the last step.”

He lifted a shoulder. “It should be.”

It should be. She recalled him saying a while back *if* they had to marry, she would win an impressive divorce settlement for her trouble. That he would actually go so far as to marry her if that was what was required to lure Erjon out of hiding.

Marry. It had never been a dream of hers. She’d never really thought relationships were in her future. She had too much to do. Too much to protect. Everything about her future had been simply keeping her and her mother safe and alive, and how could she imagine balancing all that and a life partner?

Her dreams had been so small, and Zervou had opened up a whole new world to her. Beyond survival. More than one world, really.

Not that a marriage between them would be real. Not that *this* was real or changing her dreams. If they married, it would be simply to get to Erjon. It wouldn’t be about…living beyond survival and revenge.

But too much between them had begun to feel real. Within reach. A core part of the life she wanted. The idea of marrying him wasn’t repellant, it was…intriguing.

Was she alone in that feeling? Could he behave the way he did and not care for her at all? Or was this strange pang inside of her—need and want and something deeper all wrapped up into one confusing ball of emotion—something he felt, too?

What would it be like if she let her guard down, if she let him see that she was happy, touched? That she thought the ring was beautiful and that he was good? What would happen if she risked?

What always happens to women who risk *anywhere near a powerful man.*

Destruction. Even if he was kind about it, he would say something about this not being real, and she would be the fool.

You are a fool, Ari.

She closed her eyes, trying to ice out the pain.

"Is it such a hardship, *glikí mou*, to wear a beautiful ring?" There was an edge to his voice, irritation simmering in his gaze.

She couldn't say she fully understood it or him, but she felt like she was on the edge of it making sense. Of everything or nothing making sense.

"No," she said softly, slipping the ring on her own finger. Because the ring was not the hardship.

It was loving him that would be.

CHAPTER THIRTEEN

ZERVOU DID NOT KNOW what had gotten into him. He dreamed of Ari nightly. He thought of her constantly. He could not distract himself with anything.

She was a curse.

And still, every evening he had to go parade her about. He thought he'd had a handle on it, until last night when he'd had to take her to a play with that ring on her finger. Perhaps a party or dinner would have been better, but he'd had to sit next to her in a darkened theater, where the glow of the gold on her finger matched the gold hoops in her ears.

He'd wanted to play with the ring. Twirl it around. Feel the weight of it on her finger. He'd wanted to memorize what her hand looked like with his ring on it. Perfect. Just as he'd known it would be when he'd gone to the jeweler.

It hadn't been the plan. The plan had been something outrageous. Something to get every gossip at every party, event, whatever to whisper about it.

Instead, he'd seen this vintage ring and…

Well, it didn't do to think about getting her a ring that suited her. It was just a ring. It was just money. And it got the job done regardless.

His phone rang, a welcome distraction from the frustrating circle of his thoughts. He answered, only to be shocked to hear his name in his mother's voice.

"Mother." He was surprised to hear from her. He always was. She rarely reached out herself. He had to make most overtures. They did not see eye to eye and likely never would. She wished to suffer. He did not wish her to. It was a stalemate even he could not cross.

"Zervou, thank you for taking my call."

Always so formal. So distant. Because he could never quite figure out what she wanted from him. Not help, not money. Nothing to make her life easier. But she was never happy with him staying away, either.

He simply could not make her happy, so he stayed out of her life beyond taking care of what he could without her refusal.

"Of course. Is there something I can do for you?"

There was a beat of silence, that frustrated sigh he was so used to. She'd been a warm, happy woman once. Sometimes he wondered if that vision of her he had in his mind from before his father was murdered was made up. Some trauma-induced fiction. Maybe she'd never been that woman.

But Zervou knew better. He was too much of a realist not to know better.

His father's death had broken something inside of her, and no amount of trying to mend it on his part could repair it. *He* could not repair it. Because she did not wish it to be repaired. She wanted to be broken, miserable, crushed by the weight of life and its unfairness. Sometimes, he couldn't even blame her for that.

Sometimes.

"Your grandmother has…deteriorated," Mother said

after a time. “Even the in-home nursing is not meeting her needs at this point. Our head nurse has recommended palliative care.”

He waited to feel something, but the truth of the matter was he had little to no relationship with his grandmother. She had not been a part of his childhood, having disapproved of his mother marrying his father, who had been poor. It had been a little joke when he’d been a young boy: Mama’s rich, snobby parents thumbing their nose at true love.

Some joke. Love was but a temporary thing, for his mother had loved nothing and no one since Father had died.

After the murder, Mother had refused help from her affluent family. At first, Zervou had assumed it was pride. Hurt that her family had turned its back on her for following her heart.

Eventually he’d learned whatever heart his mother had once had was long gone. He didn’t even think it was pride in her way. It was that dedication to misery. Because only when his grandmother’s health had failed did his mother go back into the family fold. Always eager to make a martyr of herself.

Zervou had been long gone by that time, since his mother wanted nothing from him. Wanted to give him nothing. So he hadn’t interfered. Only offered the necessary funds—mostly refused, occasionally accepted as a last resort.

“You have the funds at your fingertips, if you’d use them.” He tried to ensure his remaining words would not come off bitter. He knew the answer before he even asked, and still… "Would you like me to make the arrangements for you? I can arrange for the best—"

"Of course not. This is not why I called." So offended. So…familiar.

It was his turn to sigh. "Then why have you called, Mother?"

"You cannot simply throw money at this," she said, so cloaked in her disapproval.

"Then what do you require of me?" He pinched the bridge of his nose where a headache began to drum. "You have never wanted more than monetary help, and even *that* you have not wanted until you could not care for your mother yourself."

"She is your grandmother."

He'd hardly call her that, but there was no point in the old argument. "So you want me to suffer as you suffer? Tell me how. Perhaps I can pretend." *That* was bitter and pointed, but he found he could not care in the moment. Nothing he had ever done had touched his mother after his father's death, and he had no hope it ever would. Anything he offered now was a kind of…gesture to his long dead father.

"That is not what I want."

Isn't it? But he did not say this out loud. The arguments were old. Stale. He'd had to make his peace with never getting through to his mother. He'd had to make his peace with this being what they were.

Without his father, she had no love to give. And so he had lost both parents that day. It had been difficult. Perhaps there were still scars there, but he was a grown man who had learned how to deal. His money would always be available to her, but he would not drown in her misery.

She wouldn't tell him how, so how could he?

"You should be here," she told him. "You should hold her hand."

Zervou frowned. It was perhaps the first actionable directive she'd ever given him. But he did not understand it. "And what will that do? I'm not sure she would know who I am even without the dementia."

Everything went silent. It took him long seconds to realize it wasn't just his mother not speaking.

She'd ended the call.

He stared at the phone in his hand, more than a little shocked. No, they did not get along. They did not see eye to eye. But for his mother to give him a directive, then hang up…

It left him churned up. Old feelings creeping back into his mature, adult certainty that he wouldn't be bogged down by her issues.

Would things change if he booked a flight home? Would his mother be more accepting of help if he dropped everything to do what she asked now? Sit next to the grandmother he did not know, did not even like, and hold her hand as she slipped away from life?

She will never be happy. She will never accept your help.

A good reminder, but—

He heard something shuffle and looked up.

Ari.

She stood in his doorway. She was dressed for the gym, a duffel bag over her shoulder, though his ring winked on her finger. Her hair was braided back away from her face. Her skin was dewy, and she had a fresh bruise on her upper arm.

She was back from her classes and training. He hadn't realized it was quite so late. He tried to find some center within himself but found himself only at a loss for words.

"I did not mean to interrupt," she greeted, taking a hesitant step into his office. "I heard you talking, and you sounded…" She trailed off, adjusting the grip on her bag, clearly uncomfortable. "Is everything all right?"

What a question. But that wasn't what she meant. "Yes. I was simply talking to my mother." He stood behind his desk, thinking it would give him some kind of action, but instead it left him feeling even more unmoored. He looked down, unseeing, at the glossy shine of his desk. "My grandmother has taken a bit of a turn for the worse."

Ari stepped in farther, her features quickly arranged into concern. "Do you need to go see her?"

"No."

"But—"

"She is my grandmother by blood, but that is all."

Ari did not offer any arguments to that; how could she? But she did not leave. She stood there, looking like she wanted to say more.

Making him feel guilty.

Which was ridiculous. He had nothing to feel guilty about. She simply didn't know the situation.

"I have no real memory of her. She did not approve of my father and so withheld herself from my mother, our family. After my father died, she offered help, but my mother refused as she did everyone who wanted to help. It was only when the woman became sick that my mother returned to her side, and by that time I was far away."

"So why did your mother call?" Ari asked gently.

"Speaking of mothers, how does yours fare?" he asked, meeting her gaze. Holding it. Because he felt no guilt, no need to continue this conversation. He felt nothing. His mother's call was a nonissue.

But Ari frowned. And doubled down, moving closer to his desk. "Zervou. Why did your mother call if you have no relationship with your grandmother?"

He did not know why she'd push this, but if she must, what was the harm in a little truth? "Honestly? I do not know. She certainly did not want my help."

You should hold her hand. And how would that help? Any of them? No, she didn't want his help.

She wanted his pain. He understood this, more a little every year, that pain was the only currency his mother understood. And he could have drowned in that if he'd been more devoted to her, perhaps, but he'd seen no point.

Life was pain enough, why drown himself in it and become a living ghost to anyone who might care?

Not that he let anyone that close.

A strange thought in the midst of a damn strange moment. He needed to shove it away.

Like Mother always shoved you away when you tried to soothe, help, love?

"Maybe you should go, even if she didn't ask," Ari was saying around the aftershocks currently rocking his system. "Even if you don't have a relationship with your grandmother, that must be a terrible weight on your mother. She might need support herself. If you go—"

"I have offered her every conceivable help," he said, sharp and firm. "She wants none of it." A good reminder to himself as much as telling Ari.

She pressed her lips together, then took another few

steps so only the desk was between them. "Perhaps she wants your presence over what your money can buy to help, Zervou."

He laughed, low and harsh. Bitterness seemed to seep into his very bloodstream. "You do not know my mother."

"No," she agreed. "But I do know help and support do not have to mean the same thing."

He frowned at her. The words made no sense. How did one support if not with help? And if his mother wanted none of his help, what did his *support* matter? Being there solved nothing if she wouldn't allow him to take on any of the burden.

Then Ari did the oddest thing. She set her bag on the floor and skirted the desk to come stand next to him. Then, without any sort of preamble, she wrapped her arms around him.

She was warm. Her hair smelled of whatever she sprayed in it before she went to the gym in the mornings.

His heart felt heavy in his chest. An old ache stationed there, courtesy of his mother.

But with new hooks. All belonging to Ari.

Ari felt him relax, bit by bit. And so she held on. Her arms around him, her cheek pressed to his chest. Slowly, his arms came up around her too.

So they were hugging.

She'd had no real idea how to comfort him, only known that she wanted to. Needed to. Yes, things had been…a little odd between them since Paris, but she could hardly let that oddness be a reason not to offer comfort.

He'd looked so utterly lost at the idea that support and help might be two different things. And maybe he felt nothing for his grandmother, she could understand that, but she *knew* he felt complicated things for his mother.

And she wanted to help, somehow, but there was no way. So all she had to offer was support. A friendly hug. Some compassion.

She should pull away now.

But Zervou's large hand slid down her spine, and friendly and comfort began to fizzle into something else. Heat. Ache. All the things they'd been denying.

She cleared her throat and disentangled herself from him. She forced a cheerful kind of smile to beam up at him. But didn't quite manage to hold it.

Because he found her mouth with his. Hard and unyielding. Desperate, if she had to find a word for it.

She'd wanted to offer comfort, and maybe this wasn't the right way to go about it, but it felt too late now. Or maybe she'd just missed the feeling of his body on hers. It shouldn't be something she'd had long enough to miss, and yet she had. If they'd ever had…*this*.

His kiss was soft, searching, seeking. And in return she offered herself to him. Not just heat and need but the softness inside of her. Into the kiss. Into him.

Her heart ached, as if he'd landed a nasty punch to it.

Perhaps he had. Because she could not deny this love she felt for him, swamping her. Swamping the moment. It was no doubt leaking into the kiss, into him, and he would be forced to reject her.

She needed to reject it. The lesson of her life. *Don't believe in anything too good to be true.* It never was.

She pulled away, but that hurt nearly as much as the

idea of loving him did, so she kept her arms around him and pressed her forehead into this chest.

And he held her there, like it was where she belonged.

Pain erupted in her chest, hurt so much, tears filled her eyes. One even slipped over, and she moved to wipe it away quickly so he wouldn't see. It wouldn't do for him to see. Whatever she was feeling, whatever was being rearranged inside her was her own. All her feelings, always, her own. Everything her own responsibility.

But he made it seem like there was some strange world where it didn't have to be.

Luckily, she knew better. Even if she gave into this—her heart, this love she felt—she knew better than to rely on it.

"Ari." The whisper danced along her skin, but the ache inside her was her heart. "Come to bed."

She knew she would be wiser to refuse. To talk this out. Set clear boundaries, not silent ones. She knew so many things.

But she went with feeling and went to bed with him.

CHAPTER FOURTEEN

ZERVOU HAD NOT SLEPT. He'd spent an inordinate amount of time watching Ari sleep. In his bed. In his arms. With his ring on her finger still.

She had offered him comfort. Not solutions. Not arguments. Just herself.

This had never happened to him before. It was causing something to rearrange inside of him, and he did not have a good grip on it.

He had always needed a good grip. Without it, he was flung about, victim to fate's whims. He had vowed never to be again. Not after watching his father's life drain out of him. Not after watching his mother lean more fully into fate, into pain, into suffering. She wanted life to be hard to match her pain. She wanted *his* life to be hard to match her pain. And when he had not been able to do that—a child, with his own grief reaching out for something other than sadness—he had been turned away.

But Ari had not turned. She had stepped forward and offered soft. Offered sweet. Offered.

His ring. Her finger. Like she belonged to him. Like she *could*.

He'd had no plans to get married in his life, but the institution itself was no real enemy, was it? He had no shortage of money, of advantages. It wasn't as though he risked anything if they married, if they enjoyed it for as long as it was…this.

And marriage was no full binding contract, no matter what anyone said. They could be married for as long as it worked, then go their separate ways when it stopped. He wasn't so miserly that he was afraid to give her a decent divorce settlement when the time came. Why should she not have half if they decided to go their separate ways? It wouldn't hurt him any.

Yes, he supposed they could just…continue this relationship as it was after Erjon was in jail, but he liked that ring on her finger. He liked the idea of binding her to him.

If it was wrong, so be it.

It felt actionable. Sturdy. Real. Like any business deal. They could make a portion of this fake relationship real, for as long as that made sense. She could live in his house, wear his ring, be his. She could offer comfort, and she would accept his help. It would be…satisfying. Something *beyond* his revenge—just like she'd spoken about before.

What came after Erjon? Whatever they wanted. Because that was the world he'd built. One where he took what he wanted, enjoyed what he wanted and didn't martyr himself to any cause or grief.

When dawn broke, he slid from the bed. He had breakfast arranged out on the terrace, because he knew she liked that. And while she might not eat the expansive spread he offered, she would eat something. She would sit there and enjoy the view and the food.

And he stood, sipping his coffee, waiting for her, determined that whatever was next would be handled easily enough. He would arrange it to suit him. He would make the world her oyster, and she would accept the pearl inside.

He heard the door open and turned to watch her step out into the faint morning light.

"Morning," she said sleepily. She tipped her face up to the sun and took a deep breath.

He did not return her greeting, because he was struck by her. Always. And this understanding that he would never tire of exactly that. Of watching her. Of her being here. Whether *here* be his place in Corfu or anywhere else. She didn't belong any one place. She just belonged with him.

And perhaps it caused some trepidation within, but at the end of the day, he only had to convince her of the same. She was letting him take care of her, of everything. Her father, her mother. Where she lived, what she ate, how she got to work. She accepted everything from him.

Yes, there would be nothing at all wrong with getting married and seeing where that went.

"I think we should begin to plan our wedding," he said, with no preamble. And still, he watched her expression and reaction very carefully.

She stiffened, then purposefully relaxed, moving to sit at the table. She sent him a small smile. "You haven't given the engagement much time to draw him out."

"No," he agreed.

That *no* hung between them, without explanation. Without anything.

"It would not be such a hardship to be married to me,

would it, Ari?" he asked quietly. Perhaps he'd meant it to be flippant, but it hadn't come out that way.

She held his gaze, that soft thing that scared him right there in their dark depths. But he was no coward. To turn away from fear was cowardly.

She must have felt the same. She spoke softly again. "No, it would be no hardship."

"Then we shall begin to plan a wedding."

She said nothing to that. She sipped her water and looked out at the sea. He didn't interrupt whatever she was thinking about. She wasn't offering any kind of opposition, was she?

She ate a bit, and they sat in what he was determined was a companionable silence even if he felt oddly…tense.

"I never really planned on getting married," she said thoughtfully after she'd eaten a little bit, still looking out at the sea.

"Neither did I."

Her gaze moved to him. He saw a softness there he did not recognize. Something she'd kept to herself until now. Always so tough on the outside, but there was not only strength underneath. There was…whatever this was.

"So…why should that change?" she asked him. Not in challenge. No, in curiosity. "We do not need to rush into anything. I think the normal expectation is for an engagement to last. I've no doubt you can find Erjon before we'd be expected to marry."

I've no doubt. The fact she believed in him, trusted him, only added to his certainty. They would be good for one another. "We enjoy each other."

"We can enjoy one another without anything legally binding," she replied.

He tried not to be frustrated, because she was not refusing. She was simply…protecting herself. He simply needed to make it clear *he* would protect her. He would take care of everything for her. *Legally binding* was for her. "I offer you the world, Ari. Won't you take it?"

She took her time before answering, clearly considering the implications of that. "It's a lot to offer for a little enjoyment. Surely you've enjoyed other women before and not married them."

He saw in her careful study that she was searching for something, and he was determined to give it to her. To be what she needed. "Perhaps, but none so much as you."

Their gazes held, and her breath, too. The moment stretched out, a band of pressure around his chest. There were more words, more feelings. The idea of *love*. Could she love him? If she accepted all he gave her, if she let him… It could be love. Perhaps it could be love.

"All right," she said slowly, after quite a few seconds had passed. "I haven't had very much enjoyment in my life. I suppose it would be foolish to reject it out of hand."

"And you are not foolish, *glikí mou*."

She smiled softly, but he saw something not quite certain in her gaze. But she stood before he could analyze what.

"I'm sorry. I have to get to the gym. I can't be late for my class."

He nodded.

And that was how they parted. Nothing more said. No fond touches. Just…an agreement. An arrangement.

He refused to let that leave him unsettled. Perhaps they had not discussed that this was more than pretend or simple enjoyment, but they did not need to. They both knew, with or without words.

He went through the morning trying to determine what arrangements for a wedding were acceptable to make without his future bride's input. It would need to be soon, so he needed to get the ball rolling. Perhaps they could have a small affair, then something bigger and splashier for the society pages. But the ceremony itself, just for them.

So that she could become Ariadne Kritikos.

She would not need to use his name for boxing since she'd built her career as Ari Malis, but she would be his in every other arena.

It felt as right as anything ever had.

Perhaps he would take her with him to Anovol. Whether he wanted to or not, whether his mother would actually accept help or not, Zervou knew he would need to head home to deal with getting his grandmother moved into palliative care in the coming days.

Not to hold his stranger of a grandmother's hand. Not to introduce Ari to his mother, even if he was already picturing it. Even if it…somehow mattered.

He shook that thought away. He would go to handle things. Period. No matter how little it was appreciated, it was necessary. Something his father's memory demanded, no matter how Zervou wished it wouldn't.

He'd been a good man, his father. Principled. It hadn't helped him any, but still Zervou knew that at least when it came to his mother, he had to abide by *some* of the principles left behind by a man who'd died rather than bow and scrape to viciousness.

A knock sounded on his office door, and he looked up to find Bacchus there.

"There is a man from Ms. Malis's gym who is here to speak with you. A Mr. Lefteris Demo."

Zervou frowned. Ari hadn't been gone long enough for something to be wrong, had she? He didn't think so, but still concern gripped him. "Let him in."

After a few moments, Bacchus returned with a small man who looked to be in his fifties. He was dressed plainly, but he'd clearly taken some pains to look put together—his hair was slicked back, his tie was tied tight.

So this was not an impromptu meeting about Ari's well-being. No, Zervou assumed this would be about the stadium. Interesting that this man would come to him directly rather than go through Ari. Zervou respected thc move. Confident. Bold. With enough time to ensure Ari's relationship with him was not superficial.

Zervou held out his hand for the man to shake, and the return grip was strong. He looked like perhaps he'd boxed himself as a younger man.

"It is good to meet you, Mr. Kritikos. Thank you for meeting with me without an appointment."

"Of course, Mr. Demo. Come in. Have a seat, if you would."

The man nodded and moved into the large seat opposite Zervou's desk. He didn't look around in a blatant stare, but Zervou caught the considering gaze of the gold sconces, the antique tapestries. He was definitely taking stock of the wealth.

Zervou couldn't be offended by it. That was the point of a place like this, was it not?

"It is the talk of the sporting world here in Corfu that

your upcoming stadium will be quite the entertainment hub for sport."

"That is the plan."

"Boxing is popular. It could be more popular, with the right business acumen behind it. I've never been successful in that department. I understand boxing. I do not understand selling boxing to the public."

It was a smart man who knew his own weaknesses. "And I land on quite the opposite end of the spectrum. Though I try to understand any sporting event my stadium will hold, selling entertainment is my job."

"And you are the best at it in Europe it seems. Which is why I've come to you. Boxing should be a consideration for your stadium, Mr. Kritikos. And I have enough boxers, enough pull with other gyms around Greece, I could certainly outfit you with fights."

Zervou made a considering noise. He liked this man's direct nature. There were not nerves in this man. Maybe some awe, but not nerves.

"I'm sure you could, Mr. Demo, but my concern is… would enough people buy tickets to *see* these fights?"

"With the right boxer, I think they would."

"And you know the right boxer?"

Mr. Demo smiled. "We both do. It is part of why I was emboldened enough to come to you. Ari is our most talented boxer. And, as you no doubt can tell, our most… marketable. She is quite beautiful."

Zervou's hand tensed into a fist. *Beautiful* ought to be the last thing this man should be noticing about her. "I beg your pardon."

Mr. Demo held up his hands. "No disrespect. No personal interest in that way. I say so only from a business perspective. She looks good on a poster. People are intrigued to watch a beautiful woman participate in such a brutal sport. It has always been the case for her, but without backing, without international fights, I have not been able to maximize the opportunity. Her connection with you? I think could."

Zervou couldn't say he was placated, exactly. He should be. The man was speaking from a business standpoint. Zervou still did not care for it. And yet, he understood. She *would* be a draw. He'd done enough research on her before to know that she had been of interest to the greater public, but there was always something that held her back from the larger fights. The bigger stage.

It occurred to him now that Mr. Demo had mentioned international fights that likely her mother had been that obstacle. And perhaps funding. The boxing gym had certainly helped her, but it clearly didn't do enough business to really make her a star in their world.

So, her boss had come here to ask for his financial backing.

Zervou could respect it. A man did not build himself into a billionaire without being brave enough to ask for things he had no right to ask for.

"You would like to have a fight, starring Ari, at my stadium when it is done. That is what you're asking."

The man beamed at him. "Exactly. As a start. And I know a way to make such a fight draw even more ticket sales. Before your stadium's projected opening date, there is a fight in Minsk. The past few years, I've wanted to get Ari in, but we've never had the funds, and she's always been opposed to travel. But here she has been traveling with you, and you have the funds."

"Indeed, I do." Zervou leaned back in his chair. A fight in Minsk. A fight in his stadium once it was done. With his money and connections, and what he was learning about the sport area of entertainment, he could no doubt turn Ari into a star.

Was that what she wanted? He knew she wanted to succeed, but he didn't know if she wanted to be recognizable. If she wanted to be the face of something. It was a good face, though.

He'd discuss it with her tonight. Determine where a wedding would fit in. Tonight, they would discuss the future...and toast to doing it together.

"Ari did not wish to cross this line," Mr. Demo continued. "But I feel with an engagement, there is no real line left. Is there?"

For a moment, Zervou felt suspended in time.

Ari did not wish to cross this line.

He blinked at the man, whom he assumed had come behind Ari's back. Not because she didn't want him to, but because she didn't know.

She'd known.

She'd...*refused.*

Fury, white hot, scorched through him. Betrayal. This simple thing he could have done, and she had refused.

Everyone always refused.

Mr. Demo eyed him warily. Perhaps Zervou looked capable of murder in the moment. He certainly felt a kind of anger that had only ever gripped him when it came to Erjon Hyseni.

How ironic his daughter should have the same effect.

She'd *known.*

He did not let his temper loose in front of this man.

This stranger. He would not let his temper loose, period. Because what did temper matter? Only plans did, and he'd let his become derailed.

No more.

"I'm intrigued, Mr. Demo," he said, trying not to clench his jaw as he spoke. "I will take all of this information into consideration. I will let you know about my decision regarding the stadium."

"And what of sponsoring Ari for the fight in Minsk? Surely that does not require discussion with anyone."

What of it, indeed. Zervou tapped his fingers on his desk and studied the man in front of him. Then he stood, a clear sign of dismissal. "I will let you know when I have reached my decision, Mr. Demo. And not a moment before."

He hunched in the chair a bit at Zervou's icy tone but then nodded and pushed himself to his feet. "Of course. She'll win, you know. Talented girl. She'll win. It'll be a good fight for her. For us. For *you*, should you decide to sponsor her."

Zervou had no doubt all of that was true.

But Ari did not want his sponsorship. She did not want to fight in his stadium. She did not want what he could offer. Not fully. She was refusing the world on his dime, and it was worse than if she'd rejected him outright this morning. No, she'd refused his help behind his back.

And that was all he needed to know.

Ari had enjoyed the day. Her classes had gone well, her training better. She was in a pleasant mood as she slid into the car Bacchus drove after a long day.

She opened the little safe she kept her ring in and slid it on her finger. She liked the weight of it. The look of it.

Married.

She still couldn't quite get over the way Zervou had brought that up. Not lightly. There'd been an intensity to him this morning.

Ari knew better than to hope. She knew better than to believe in something that clearly was too good to be true. Maybe Zervou was letting her think there was more to this than there was or maybe he even felt this too. Maybe, in the moment, he was serious.

But it wouldn't last. *Enjoyment* was hardly the same thing as love.

She swallowed at the little lump that formed in her throat. That was all right, though. Nothing had changed really. Maybe her feelings, but in the end, this was just another *enjoy what she could while she could* moment. Always knowing that on the other side of it she would be going back to the way her life had been. Nothing was permanent. She was in charge of herself.

Even if he wanted to get married.

She squeezed her left hand. *Enjoy the moment as it was given. Take some luxury.* If it made it harder to do without later on, so be it.

It would be hard no matter what, to lose him from her life. So quickly he'd become an anchor to it. A safe place. He wanted to give her the world, and she could not trust it…but she wanted to. Moreso after yesterday. Comforting him when he had been hurting had meant something to her. She could give him something, just as he gave her so much.

A risk? Yes. So be it if it meant, for a little while, she might be his wife.

The thought filled her with a longing she didn't quite know what to do with.

She got out of the car when Bacchus pulled up in front of the house. She walked inside. Like this was hers. Like she belonged. Zervou had made it feel that way.

"Mr. Kritikos would like to see you in his office," Bacchus told her as he came up behind her.

She frowned a little at that. His office? Odd. Still she dumped her bag and went to find him. Usually when she returned from the gym, he was ready for whatever public appearance they had that night. Tonight was supposed to be some charity gala, if she recalled.

She had a beautiful dress all laid out and was looking forward to another delicious meal she didn't have to cook herself.

But when she arrived at his office, the door was closed. She hesitated for a moment. Something seemed… strange. She shook her head. She was being ridiculous. Still, when she reached out for the doorknob, she couldn't quite get herself to turn and push the door open.

She knocked instead.

After a moment, she heard Zervou's voice rumble from behind the door to come in.

Because you're being ridiculous. She wiped damp palms against her sweatpants and chided herself on already looking for problems where they didn't exist.

When she stepped inside, he sat behind his desk. He was dressed exactly as he'd been when she'd left, and when she entered there was no smile. No greeting.

He looked her up and down. There was no heat there. No emotion at all, really. Just a cold kind of calculation.

Something was *very* wrong, and that was not in her imagination at all.

She did not recognize this expression. She would have said it reminded her of when they first met, except she could see beyond that arrogant mask to the lick of fury.

He was angry about something, even if he hid it well.

"Is something wrong?" she asked. She never could quite ignore the underlying emotion in a room, even when perhaps it would serve her well.

There was a pregnant pause. He tapped his fingers on his desk, then slowly rose. But he stayed locked behind his large desk. "Your Mr. Demo came to see me today."

Lefteris… "He did what?" Her own anger swelled quickly. After she'd told him no. After he'd pretended to understand her stance on integrity. He'd gone to Zervou behind her back. Because asking for him to sponsor a fight for her was the only reason he could have come here.

The bastard.

"He should not have done that, Zervou. I apologize. I asked him not to."

Zervou did not immediately soften or accept her apology. His demeanor remained exactly the same. "And why did you ask him not to?"

Her eyebrows drew together. "What do you mean? It was not appropriate for him to use my connection to you assume kind of…greased wheel toward using you."

"That is business, Ariadne. Greased wheels and using."

A frown tugged at the corners of her mouth. She didn't understand what he was trying to say, but it didn't matter. "But this isn't business. It is my career."

"And that is where you draw the line at my help?"

"Yes," she said simply, because it was that simple.

She saw this was the wrong answer as the fury in his eyes leapt, as his hands clenched into fists. But she did not understand. "What do you have to be angry about? He went around me. *I* told him no when he asked. He never should have—"

"I have no right to be angered by this *no* you gave him, without discussing it with me?"

"Angered?" She shook her head, trying to understand him. "Absolutely not. Boxing is mine. This was my choice, and he did not respect it. Why should *you* be angry at *me*?"

"Because I would give you this. It would be nothing for me to fund all these things. And you refuse?"

"I didn't *refuse*. I did not think it appropriate to ask. You have already given me too much. Our goals may be the same, but I will not ask for more when you have already given me so much."

He made a dismissive kind of noise and turned away from her, both things that stoked her anger hotter.

"I have integrity," she told him, fisting a hand to her heart. "I have pride. You will not dismiss these things."

"Pride," he spat, whirling to face her. "You have stubbornness."

"There are some things in life that…it matters to earn them. Not just have them handed to you. Just because you *could* do something doesn't mean I want you to. You have no right to be angry about this."

"No, of course not." Each word was an icy dagger.

She did not understand his extreme reaction to this.

Or she wouldn't have, if she hadn't heard him speak of his mother last night. His frustration and disgust over her refusal of his help. She blinked at her own realization. Was it so simple? Such an easy corollary? Maybe, maybe not. But it was the defense she needed.

"I am not your mother," she told him very softly, with clear, precise control.

His head snapped back like she'd punched him. The fury turned into something else. Something that had her own ebbing away, because…

"No, but you women are all the same, are you not?" he said, vicious and cold.

"You women," she repeated, shock and fury twining in her system a dangerous concoction. "Here are your true colors then. Lumping women together because they do not ask how high when you demand they jump."

"Ah, so here it is. What you really think of me."

"What I really think of you?" She furiously blinked back the tears in her eyes. "I *thought* you understood. I thought…" *I thought you loved me.* Foolish girl that she was. No matter how she'd tried to talk herself out of it, she'd really thought there was something real here. Or could be.

Instead, she was just another possession in a powerful man's quest for more. And when she didn't shine in the precise right way, she was relegated to…something else. Something subhuman. A pawn.

"I will be gone the next two days," he said, his anger

and fury tamped down into something icy and sharp. "You should be gone when I return."

Gone. It ripped through her, the implications of that. Gone. He wanted her gone.

She would not cry, because she'd known, hadn't she? No amount of soft feelings or talk of enjoyment or marriage or giving her the world could change the very simple fact that this was the basic truth of life.

Love was not real. Pain, suffering and selfishness were real. *This* was never meant to be real, and it was her fault for mixing it up enough to be hurt by that.

"What of my father?" She tried to keep the squeak out of her voice, but her throat seemed to be closing up. That was why she was even here in the first place.

"I have the necessary leads. I'll snuff him out. He'll pay. You have no need for me, Ariadne. You have made this clear. So I have no need for you."

Which wasn't fair. "No, I have *not.* You have decided that not wanting you to warp this one thing that is mine, that I have built myself, that is who I am, is some kind of refusal. You have decided that it means all women are your mother. That is *your* choice, not anything I made clear."

She could see she wasn't getting through to him. He was angry and stubborn and…wrong. Just *wrong.* And she could not fix that for him. She felt weak for letting a tear fall, but she couldn't seem to help it. Still, when she delivered her parting shot, she was proud of how icy and distanced her tone felt.

She took the ring off her finger, placed it firmly on the desk between them and met his gaze. "Seek therapy,

Zervou," she said, then whirled on her heel and stalked out of the room.

She didn't fully cry until she left the premises.

And then she was afraid she might never stop.

CHAPTER FIFTEEN

He had seethed. He had instructed his staff what to do. Eradicate any and all evidence Ariadne Malis had ever been in his estate. In his *life.* His security detail would still watch after her, from afar, until her father was behind bars, but he would have nothing to do with her.

Nothing.

He'd considered rescinding funding for her mother's stay in Mykonos, but it felt a step too far. He'd have a discussion with Maria's case manager regarding her current status and go from there. He hoped Ari choked on the help she was forced to take.

But he could not worry about that now. He had his own demons to fight.

The plane could not touch down near enough to Anovol to suit Zervou. He would have to drive nearly an hour to reach his mother. An hour of time spent thinking, stewing and dreading what his future looked like now that Ari would not be in it.

He supposed the one positive there was that it kept him from thinking about his mother.

Until his car pulled up to the tiny house—a cottage really. It was well-kept. He'd made certain of that whether she'd liked it or not. The nurse was paid by him, after all, so if she noted a leak in the roof or issues with the plumbing, she informed him. And he sent someone along to fix it, with instructions to ignore whatever protests his mother put up. If she got too insistent, he worked with the nurse to ensure Mother was in the village shopping when the repairs needed to be done.

Otherwise she would live in a hovel. Even with his grandmother, she would suffer. Just to fucking suffer.

He pounded on the door and waited for an answer. When the door creaked open, it was not a nurse, but his mother who answered.

Of course, she must do everything herself.

Lines sat heavy on her face. She was too thin. Always too thin. But her dark eyes registered something akin to relief to mix with the surprise. "Zervou," she greeted. Her mouth curved—it was not a smile. He'd long since believed the gravity of his father's death did not allow his mother to smile. But it was some expression of happiness. "You have come."

"Not to hold anyone's hand. To handle the arrangements," he told her tersely. "Is the head nurse available? I'd like to speak with her." He moved past his mother into the tiny, cramped kitchen. Everything neat as a pin.

His mother would have it no other way. She would have scrubbed that floor on her hands and knees after every draining day.

"I told you that I did not require your *assistance*. I simply thought—"

"You thought I might like to scrape myself over the coals with you. I do not. What is the nurse's name again? Penelope, wasn't it?" He would move through the small amount of rooms until he found her. “Probably deserves a raise,” he muttered to himself.

“Yes, throw money at it. That is always your answer, is it not?”

He stopped on a dime. Turned to face his mother. She had always been so disdainful of the thing he had worked so hard to do. She had never once taken it as it was intended. To help. To ease. He had built his wealth himself, and she had no use for it. *No one does.*

“The money you resent so much has eased your life, your burdens,” he told her coldly. “It could do more, help more, if you would let it.” This was always the conversation, the argument. It never changed. No matter how old he got, how much he had, how hard he tried, they always ended up right back here.

He should never have come. Why had he let his anger eradicate that clear truth?

“Yes, it is my fault for wanting more from you.”

He snorted his derision. Childish, perhaps, but it was all he had in the moment. “You want *nothing* from me.”

He had never said that. Never truly let himself think it, but it was true. Starker in this moment because he was forced to realize… Ari was *not* like his mother. She had taken help, comfort. Offered the same right back. Not in everything, no, but in some things. In the emotional things.

He shook that thought away. This wasn’t about Ariadne. It was about his mother. But in the contrast, he saw things clearer. “You want nothing from anyone. You want to be alone in your misery and martyrdom.”

Mother gathered herself, straightened shoulders and lifted chin. She looked up at him with that icy glare he recognized so well from a childhood spent begging her to let someone, anyone, help.

Except then he'd been shorter than her, weaker than her. Desperate for her love, her comfort, when his entire world had been upended.

But she'd only seen her world. Then. Now. Amazing that even being a grown man could not fix this.

"I did not *choose* misery. Misery was done to me. I suppose you could never love so deeply that such a loss would leave a mark," Mother said with such icy disdain.

Love. What was love but a disease? The loss of it—always inevitable—had turned his mother into this. And him into an aching wound he couldn't seem to stop. Because here he was dealing with his mother and thinking of Ari.

But he refused to think of Ari here. He refused to think of love, because it had been *enjoyment.* It had been simple. It had been give and receive.

Is that not what you want from love?

Didn't matter. He hadn't come here for any give or take. He'd come to ensure his grandmother's move into the palliative care center some fifty kilometers away.

"I will move her," his mother said, hurrying in front of him, like she would block his way. "I will handle this. You need do nothing except say your goodbyes."

"Explain to me, Mother, why I should say goodbye to a woman who means nothing to me?" He looked down at his mother then and saw that she really couldn't understand his position. "Explain to me why she should mean anything to you when she turned her back on you. When you would not accept her help when she turned back to you after Father died."

"Your father was *murdered.* He did not die. He was *killed.*"

"Yes, I was there, too, if you recall."

She turned away from him then. As she had after that day. Always turning away from what she had left, so dedicated to that which was gone. His father. Her mother—because even if she was alive, her mind and memories had long since gone.

And Zervou had to admit that he'd come here for this. To see her turn away. To throw himself into this continued rejection. Because it was familiar. Because he wanted to prove to himself that Ari had done the same and she had deserved being cast out.

Instead, he saw his mother casting out that which she should have loved, cared for, cherished, and he felt shamed.

Ari hadn't wanted nothing from him. After all, she had comforted him. She had dined with him, spent time in his bed. She had taken his ring and agreed to marry him.

The one thing she'd denied him had been a hand in her boxing. And while it still felt like betrayal, with some distance, with this stark difference between the two women shoved in his face, he realized that…she wasn't wrong.

She had wanted one thing to be her own. She had needed to trust her own pride and integrity. For her work, for herself. It wasn't about him.

It was a strange realization. Because his mother's issues weren't about him, either, no matter how they hurt him.

The similarity in these women was only the similarity in the fact they'd made choices for themselves.

But his mother had never thought of him—or if she had once, it had been lost with his father. Ari had accepted his help. No, not all of it. But she had not refused him wholesale. She had, as she said, made her choices. She had taken what she felt she could live with. For her pride. Her integrity.

Things he had esteemed her for. Things he had himself and understood, but only when it came to himself. He had not extended that understanding to her, because…

Refusal triggered some primal, childish anger in him. It shamed him, here in the aftermath of that same primal, childish anger. Or maybe it wasn't so much childish as a result of being a helpless child, traumatized by the violent loss of his father. And never helped. Only told to suffer.

Ari had suffered, too. At her father's hand. At her mother's. But she was not married to her misery as his mother was. No, Ari was not miserable. She did not blame the world around her for everything. She did not blame those who could not measure up to her sainthood for her pain.

She had not spent her life building an empire meant only to take down her enemy. Erjon had done terrible things to her and the mother she loved, but Ari had built herself something not just to protect her mother or herself, but because she had a passion for it. Yes, most of her life had been centered on survival, on taking care of her mother, but boxing was the thing she'd carved out as *hers*.

Zervou came to the realization he had nothing like that. Not until Ari had come into his life and opened up some new part of him. He had lived his life with a dogged commitment to ruining Erjon. No relationships except working ones or superficial ones. Always just out of reach. Never giving. Never taking.

Just like his mother.

Until Ari.

Perhaps he could not understand why her integrity meant he could not fund her dreams, but…she had been right to call him out for lumping her in with his mother.

Mother wasn't refusing his help. She was choosing her misery. He had always linked them, but Ari had shown him a different way. Something…more balanced, he supposed.

She had told him, outright, hadn't she? Support and help were not the same. He wanted them to be. But he could not make that the case for anyone. Not his mother. Not Ari. And he had to admit, in this moment, that it was fair.

Perhaps Ari should have been more upfront with him about not wanting his influence in this thing that was her own, but their relationship hadn't been *real*, had it? Even when it had been, he hadn't told her. He'd simply told her they would marry. That he enjoyed her. Keeping that careful distance.

Like right now he was telling his mother he would handle things.

He never told her why.

So he looked at her now—standing there with her back to him. Stiff and closed off. But he did not have to be.

"If Father had not been killed, he would be here, holding onto some of these burdens for you. He would have provided for you, as I have tried to do. *That* is what I have tried to do."

His mother turned slowly, looking at him a bit like he was a ghost. "But your father is gone."

Zervou sighed. There was no getting through to her. That was the only pillar in her life. Her loss.

He could not fix that for her.

But he could fix himself.

"I will handle the arrangements, though I know you will not appreciate this. I do it for you, though you'd rather feel the misery of it. Perhaps at some point you will want something else. Perhaps you will not. I will continue to help where I can, and I will continue to live my life in the pursuit of something more than the misery of losing him. If you are ever ready for that, you only need contact me."

She said nothing. Not ready yet. Perhaps not ready ever.

But Zervou was ready. Ready to turn a page.

Ari won her fight.

The one she'd trained so hard for, even while eating decadent meals and spending evenings on Zervou's arm.

The win should have come with triumph. Delight. Excitement. The attention she would garner might be enough to get someone—*aside* from Zervou—interested in sponsoring her fight in Minsk.

Or so Lefteris said. Ari couldn't seem to manage to care. It still came from the interest people had in her because of Zervou, and while that might not hurt her integrity any, right now it hurt her heart.

So she simply wanted to be alone with her aches and pains and this empty pit inside of her that had swept away any satisfaction or pride.

She wanted to cry.

She wished he'd been here. To see her. To cheer her on. Just days ago, that was exactly what he would have done.

She could blame him fully for the change in their circumstance except…while she had not been wrong in anything she had said, she had been wrong in keeping a few things to herself.

She should have told him that she loved him, not just *enjoyed* him. She should have stood up and said that she wanted his ring to be real and their future to be for them, not to capture her father.

Perhaps the outcome would have been the same, perhaps he could only see everything as his mother's refusals, but it had been cowardice to keep it to herself. To not go for broke.

She moved into the locker room, thanking people for their congratulations and trying to find a second alone to think.

Now that the fight was over, there was nothing else to do.

Or so she thought, because as she stepped into the locker room, eager to slip into the ice bath and forget all else, she was met with a figure she might not have recognized.

He seemed shorter, heavier than he'd been the last time he'd seen him. His hair had thinned, though he tried to hide it with creative combing.

"Father." She looked around. How had he possibly gotten in here? She was too aware of her surroundings not to know Zervou's security detail still watched after her. But somehow Erjon must have slipped by them.

"The time has come, *malko momichentse*."

Little girl. How ridiculous. "I cannot imagine what time you mean," she returned. He was inside the locker-room, and she was at the door. It would have been simple to step right back out. It would be simple to run.

She had too much pride for that.

"I know where your little boyfriend is. Off visiting his mother in that hovel of a village I once ruled."

Congratulations, you win, she wanted to say to him. But she didn't.

"Now, with no protector, you will come with me."

Ari laughed. Not even in an effort to offend him. It was just the most ridiculous thing in the world that he thought she would simply *go* with him. "No, Erjon. Not on the list of things happening today."

"And if I pull my weapon?"

Her laughter might have died, but she didn't let her fear show. "I'm willing to bet, even after already fighting my heart out, I could have you disarmed before you could do anything with it."

"You think I can't fight?" he demanded, his cheeks already mottled red. "You think I haven't defended myself all these years?"

"Defended?" She laughed with all the acid churning in her stomach. "All you've ever done with those fists is instigate and harm. Actually, I imagine even that isn't true. You hide behind weapons bought by someone else. You have always tried to make me your little pawn because it is all *you* are, all *you'll* ever be."

He sneered, taking a threatening step toward her. But that was the goal. The closer he was, the more likely she was able to stop him from grabbing a weapon from inside his coat.

"I *am* a weapon," he told her viciously. And clearly believed it. "No pawn."

But Ari refused to. "You are a hiding coward."

He lunged forward, but she easily dodged the blow. She knew she could outfight him, though she did worry he'd get to whatever weapon he was carrying under his jacket. She might not be able to fight that.

But she wouldn't run. Everything she'd fought for these past ten years would not let her run. So she took two quick steps forward, feinted left, then landed an uppercut square to the jaw.

It sent him sprawling. Though her fist ached at doing so without a glove, especially after already taking the abuse of a fight, satisfaction was like a drug.

She moved toward him, but he'd gotten quickly to his feet. This time when she feinted, he must have seen it.

The blow was a shock. He'd gotten some decent power behind it, and she saw stars as she stumbled back.

"You were promised long ago, and I must keep my promises if I wish to keep my life." He was reaching inside of his jacket, and she couldn't let him grab whatever he had.

She charged. She did not let fear or hate control her. Luckily, the control of the fight was still in her. So she landed her blows that he could not sufficiently block, and she sent him sprawling again. This time, he stayed down.

He was laid out on the floor, blood dribbling from his mouth.

There was a sudden commotion all around her, but she couldn't quite pay attention to it. All her attention was going into staying standing.

He'd waited until after the fight so she'd be weak, hurting, exhausted. And he'd still lost.

She spit the blood out of her mouth next to him, breathing heavily. "You will rot in jail, and I will celebrate every day of your imprisonment."

Then she was being jostled out of the way by…well, by police. How had so many known to come, she wondered. Then she turned slightly to see Bacchus.

But not just him. Zervou stood next to him.

Ari blinked. Was she hallucinating?

Once Erjon had been dragged out of the room, she sank onto the bench, legs suddenly watery. Eyes filled with tears. But she could not let them fall.

Not in front of Zervou. Who stood before her now. Silent and foreboding. *Beautiful.*

Oh, she really was pathetic.

Bacchus talked in low tones with a police officer by the door, but Ari couldn't manage to focus enough to hear what they were saying. Not with Zervou standing there.

"When did you return?" she asked, trying to sound casual but not able to meet his gaze. "I thought you weren't going to be here." She jutted her chin to where Erjon had been dragged. "He didn't think you were here."

"I watched your fight," he said softly. "Then came back just in time to see you land the final blow on him."

Because it infuriated her, she looked up at him now. "And you did not step in to land it yourself? How novel."

His sigh was soft, but he did not say anything to that. He carefully crouched before her so they were eye to eye. He lifted a washcloth to her mouth, then gently wiped away what she imagined was blood.

"You were doing fine on your own. You usually do, whether you need to or not."

So he had learned nothing, and was here to what? Fight? "Yes, that is what survivors do, Zervou. You claim to know what that is like, but I am not altogether sure. Perhaps you have become so insulated by your power and your money you have made everyone else the problem, when you are the only one *I* see."

Which was, of course, a lie. Her father was a bigger problem than anything Zervou had done to her. What was a little broken heart, after all? At least he'd broken it when she had a full stomach.

"Are you hurting me because you hate me, Ari?" he asked softly. "Or because you are hurting?"

She eyed him then, not quite certain of his tone. His gentleness. "Can't it be both?"

His eyes met hers as he held out the cloth to Bacchus, who took it and then put an ice pack in Zervou's hand. Zervou lifted it to her cheek.

"It would wreck me if you should actually hate me, *glikí mou*."

She blinked once, winced a little at the pain there, even with the ice pack on it. *Wreck.* What a dramatic word. Perhaps she had a concussion. "Why are you here?" she asked him, about to lose the battle with tears.

"I went to see my mother. You were not wrong. I could only see your refusal as…refusal of everything I wanted to give. Because she has refused it all. I was wrong, to put that on you."

The threat of tears didn't stop, but an awful wriggle of hope bloomed in her chest. He was admitting he was wrong? Zervou?

"I want to make your life easy. I want to handle everything for you, because I love you."

She sucked in a breath. *Love.* She had never believed in such a thing beyond the responsibility she felt for her mother. The symbiotic and somewhat tragically codependent relationship born of poverty, trauma and necessity.

Zervou had allowed her to believe in something else. And now he was saying he loved her.

But she couldn't be certain he understood. If love was just a cage…

But before she could try to fight past the lump in her throat, he continued, "Ever since my father was killed, she chose her misery. And whether I was aware of it or not, I have spent all this time trying to take it away. Trying to take care of her. Because I love her as well. But she will not allow it. For so long, I internalized this as my failure."

Ari was shaking her head before she even realized it.

"No, it is not mine," he said, and she realized she was crying because with the hand that did not hold the ice pack, he wiped the moisture off her other cheek. "It took you… We have worked as partners to draw your father out. And look—we succeeded. Because I gave, and you took. Because I took when you gave, even if I did not recognize it at the time. I saw this one thing you refused as a failure, as *my* failure, and so I lashed out. And so I destroyed. But I was wrong, and I am sorry."

Ari had long loved someone who had failed her, and the pain of that lived in her even as she strove to forgive her mother for a disease she could not control.

But Zervou had not failed her. "You made a mistake.

An honest one, born of your issues. And now you seek to fix it. I would also like to fix my mistake."

"Ari—"

"I do not wish for you to sponsor my boxing, because I wish that to be something I did on my own. Whether this is right or wrong, I do not know, but it is important to me. Almost as important as what I should have said before. I love you, Zervou. This thing between us has turned into something real and important. And I should very much like to marry you, to love you. To…work together, to help each other and to support each other when we need to do our own thing."

His gaze met hers. Emotion swam there. Love swam there. That thing she had trouble identifying these past few weeks.

Love.

And it was funny how her father had been taken away, and Zervou would no doubt ensure he was jailed forever. But the satisfaction of that waned in comparison to the joy she felt when Zervou gently placed his lips to her throbbing ones.

"If that is a proposal, *glikí mou*, I accept." He got to his feet and drew her up with him. "Come, Ari. Let me take care of you, and then we will celebrate."

She leaned on him as he led her out of the locker room. "What will we be celebrating? My win? Erjon in jail?"

"Us," he said emphatically.

Because *us* was more important than everything else.

EPILOGUE

"LET ME HOLD the baby."

Zervou handed off the squirming, whimpering almost one-year-old to Maria.

"There now, Grandma will make it all better," she cooed at young Ioannis.

Normally Zervou preferred to ease his son's frustrations himself, but his nerves couldn't quite settle enough to do so.

"I still don't know that a sporting arena is any place for a baby," Maria muttered irritably. But she smoothed out her tone. "But you will see Mama win, won't you?" She held Ioannis up so he put his weight on his pudgy little feet and bounced on her legs. This eased any complaints he'd had about being restrained.

Nothing could ease the twists and turns in Zervou's chest. Nothing, until this fight was over.

Ari had put a lot into coming back after the birth of their son. She had determined this comeback fight would be her last. Win or lose.

He wanted her to win, and he had absolutely no say in the manner. No matter that his stunningly successful stadium boasted the fight, only Ari and her opponent could determine the outcome.

It had been quite the lesson.

Ari had been quite the lesson.

Ioannis, family, love had been quite the lesson. He had continued to learn it, and so had Ari. It was no easy task, even with love. But it was the most worthwhile task.

Maria was doing well. His own mother had met Ioannis, and while there were still many inroads to be made, for the first time since his father's death, Zervou saw a glimmer of love and life in his mother's eyes.

Hope.

And while they lived and loved, Erjon rotted in prison. Exactly where he belonged.

Ari appeared in the ring, as did her opponent, but Zervou only had eyes for his wife. He watched her ready, then watched the bout, heart in his throat. She fought as she always did, with brains and heart and determination.

And he knew, in this moment, she was saying goodbye to an angry young girl who'd been harmed and struggled and *survived.* This was her goodbye to survival.

And stepping into what was next.

It took eight rounds. But finally, her opponent went down and was counted out. Cheers erupted form the stadium below them.

"Mama!" Ioannis shrieked excitedly. Unlike many small children, he loved the noise of the crowd.

"Yes, Mama," Zervou agreed. "Mama won."

They stayed in their private box. Ari would come to them when she was ready. It felt like hours, though it wasn't. When she arrived, freshly showered and bandaged up, she was beaming.

Zervou scooped Ioannis up so he wouldn't make a

beeline for Ari until she was ready. He crossed the room to her.

She swayed a little, but he caught her, and she leaned against them, reaching out to hold Ioannis's outstretched hand.

She sighed, exhausted and bruised but clearly satisfied. Happy as she leaned, basking in her win on her own two feet and the family who'd helped her get there.

"So, you will go out on top, *glikí mou.*" He kissed the top of her head. "I always knew you would."

Steadier now, she took Ioannis's weight, though she still leaned into Zervou. She pressed a kiss to their son's forehead.

"Perhaps I did, and I am proud. But the best is yet to come." She smiled up at him, and he knew it to be true.

With love and family by his side, the best was always yet to come.

* * * * *

Were you blown away by the drama in
Greek's Hand in Vengeance*? Then why not explore*
these other sensational stories by Lorraine Hall!

A Wedding Between Enemies
Pregnant, Stolen, Wed
Unwrapping His Forbidden Assistant
Secretly Pregnant Princess
King's Heir Ultimatum

Available now!